SLEIGHTLY NERVOUS

Trying not to overdo my clumsiness, I performed a single cut and passed the deck back to John, letting him square it. "Five-card draw," he announced and began flicking cards to each of us.

I knew my first card was the King of Hearts before I even peeked at it. When cutting the deck, I had crimped the corner of the King of Hearts and left it at the bottom on the deck. But John had other plans for it and made sure it ended up in front of me. Starting with the very first hand, John was dealing off the bottom. With flawless technique.

As he continued to deal, my hand crept over my tie clasp. I slowly swiveled my seat back and forth, snapping pictures of everyone.

The game had begun.

Avon Books are available at special quantity discounts for bulk purchases for sales promotions, premiums, fund raising or educational use. Special books, or book excerpts, can also be created to fit specific needs.

For details write or telephone the office of the Director of Special Markets, Avon Books, Dept. FP, 105 Madison Avenue, New York, New York 10016, 212-481-5653.

SLEIGHTLY GUILTY

PATRICK A. KELLEY

AVON BOOKS ◆ NEW YORK

SLEIGHTLY GUILTY is an original publication of Avon Books. This work has never before appeared in book form. This work is a novel. Any similarity to actual persons or events is purely coincidental, except for the universally recognized magicians and sleight-of-hand artists who are mentioned in passing.

AVON BOOKS
A division of
The Hearst Corporation
105 Madison Avenue
New York, New York 10016

First Avon Books Printing: May 1988

AVON TRADEMARK REG. U.S. PAT. OFF. AND IN OTHER COUNTRIES, MARCA REGISTRADA, HECHO EN U.S.A.

Printed in the U.S.A.

K—R 10 9 8 7 6 5 4 3 2 1

For Eleanor Wilson Maurer,
a great teacher.
She taught so many of us that entertainment
is both a serious and a fun business.

CHAPTER ONE

The faded sign above the warehouse entrance featured a jumbo chocolate bar and the words *Buntnell's Candyland—Wholesalers*. Although the parking lot was deserted, the inside of the building buzzed with employees filling orders. All transactions at Candyland were strictly cash, and the merchandise was carefully packed in gaily colored candy boxes. Every once in a while, some of the boxes actually contained candy.

I jittered my fingernails on the countertop, trying to hurry the man waiting on me. He was studying my shopping list as if it were a problem in Einsteinian physics. All I wanted was to make my purchases and get the hell out before they discovered I was an outsider. The life of a woman named Cate depended on it.

Although it was located just across town, Candyland seemed light-years away from the Mystic Isle nightclub, where I was currently performing. For the past two weeks I had been trying out a new ending for my act: after being shackled in a hundred pounds of chains, I then vanished from the stage in a cloud of smoke, only to reappear a few seconds later in the back of the audience. The crowds might not remember my name anymore, but they did remember that trick.

Earlier today, I had taken a private tour of the town of Parrish, Pennsylvania, catching sights that the Chamber of Commerce—proud of the sumptuous summer homes and the nearby mountain resorts—would never admit existed.

I began my journey on the steps of a boarded-up church, talking to an old man who was drinking a bottle of wine so cheap that to hide it in a paper bag would have given it too much dignity. He gave me directions to a corner newsstand. The owner of the newsstand referred me to a bar where the jukebox played in hoarse whispers and the customers shot pool on stained tables. After listening sympathetically to my story, the man washing glasses behind the bar told me that Buntnell's Candyland was the place to buy what I wanted. He even supplied me with a few names to get me past the doorman. "After that," he said, "you're on your own." I chuckled, telling him I'd been on my own a lot longer than that.

A couple of flimsy lies—told with a glibness that comes only from telling lies for a living—had gotten me past the doorman. After a moment of scrutiny, he waved me inside with his thumb and then resumed his game of solitaire. If he had given my story any thought at all, my life expectancy would have equaled that of the proverbial snowball in hell.

Now, a big, soft man named Skip was standing behind the counter in the candy warehouse, running his finger down my list. He made clucking noises at certain items, indicating that he either didn't stock them or he couldn't read my writing. He wore a brown apron that strained to cover his sagging paunch, evidence of his tendency to sample the merchandise. After every puff, he held his juicy cigar stub out in front of him as though its pungency offended even him. Mixing uneasily with the cigar smoke was the heavy aroma of malted milk balls and bubble gum.

The inside of the concrete building reminded me of a flea market. Boxes with taped price tags were piled everywhere. On either side of me I could hear customers haggling excitedly over prices. There were no cash registers, just a few cigar boxes behind the counter that were overflowing with dollar bills.

"I don't know what to tell you, buddy," Skip finally said, snapping my list between his fingers. "This stuff you want is specialized. Not the kind of thing we usually keep lying around. If you got a few days, we can make everything up for you. Of course, I could set you up right now with a couple decks of readers or maybe a handful of tops." He let my paper flutter down to the counter and looked at me with watery eyes.

Great, I thought. This is all I need. A test. Ordinarily, I'd gladly show him that I knew what I was talking about. I'd demonstrate how a deck of cards in the proper hands can obey their master like a blue-ribbon winner at a kennel show. But time was crowding me, and even the best magician in the world couldn't stop the inexorable ticking of the clock on the wall behind Skip.

I glanced at the other customers. To my right, a nebbish-looking man in a topcoat was taking solemn inventory of eight cardboard boxes, all bearing the name of Smooth-O's, the Marshmallow Nougat Treat. He fingered through the contents of each box until he found what he was looking for: several plastic packets of white powder wedged in among the candies. A little ''sugar'' to help the Smooth-O's go down even smoother.

On my left stood a burly, humorless man who didn't bother concealing his purchase under the cover of candy. From inside his coat, he slid out a pistol with a barrel so long it seemed to take several seconds to clear his lapels. He picked up a metal tube from the counter and calmly twisted it onto the barrel, like a plumber fitting a piece of pipe. He cased the warehouse until his eyes settled on a decades-old calendar pinup taped to the cinder-block wall behind the counter. The woman in the picture was wearing a one-piece bathing suit that unfortunately covered entirely too much of her body. She was sitting on the hood of a T-Bird with her long legs crossed. The man took careful aim and squeezed the trigger. Anticipating a bang, I hunched my shoulders, but the only sound was the hammer clicking on an empty chamber. He dry-fired several more times. I leaned toward him and said, ''That silencer sure is a smart investment. Now your target practice won't have to disturb the other tenants in your apartment.''

He didn't smile, but he did shake his head in grudging admiration, as though my joking had taken great courage.

I turned back to Skip, deciding that indignation was my best ploy. ''How dare you try to stick me with bush-league equipment? You'd probably try to sell training wheels to the Hell's Angels. Everyone knows you need tinted glasses to see the marks on the back of reader cards—you want me to go to my game tonight looking like I just stepped out of a 3-D movie? And what's the deal with these tops? Even if I were a dice worker, I sure as hell wouldn't use them. I've seen more than one slob end up with his knuckles in a vise after rolling too many sevens and elevens. For crissakes, Skip, you think I'm playing with a bunch of fraternity punks tonight?''

Skip raised a corner of his mouth in a half-smile. ''Sorry. I can't give you what I don't have.''

The man with the pistol, still concentrating on the pinup, clicked off another empty round. Noting that he lacked the vacant, marbly eyes of so many in his profession, I took a chance.

I clamped my fingers around Skip's wrist and yanked him half-way across the counter. The man with the boxes of Smooth-O's wrapped his arms around his candy like a protective father. I glanced back at the doorman in time to see the cards from his solitaire game sputter from his hands. With one smooth motion he stood up and whipped his hand through the air, as though catching a fly. His fingers stopped a quarter of an inch from the opening of his coat. Waiting to see what I did next, he cleared his throat, and it had the effect of a drill sergeant barking a command. Activity in Candyland suddenly halted as customers looked up from their goods and warehousemen stopped wheeling their dollies. Clerks dropped their boxes and clustered together to watch the show. Center stage was now mine, and I felt quite at home.

Pointing at the man with the silencer on his pistol, I said, "What kind of place is this, Skip? The national finals in the Twenty-five-Meter-Rapid-Fire-with-Silencer Competition are coming up soon, and this gentleman is concerned that his new accessory might throw off his aim. Yet what do you give him to aim at? Nothing but a lousy calendar. Why don't we give him something more natural, Skip? Something he's more used to? Hey, I got it! Why don't we use you, Skip? How about sitting down and pretending you're eating in a restaurant and all your bodyguards have just gone to the lavatory and—"

The man hefted his gun from one hand to the other. Skip's body stiffened, and he waited in dread to see how the customer would react. It was as though I had insulted royalty. I thought, What did I get myself into? What if the big guy simply purchases one bullet from Skip and then gives it to me as a present—at twelve hundred feet per second? But the man with the gun slapped the counter and let out a short, gruff laugh. Then the man with the Smooth-O's laughed. And the doorman dropped his hand to his side and laughed. Finally, Skip jumped on the laughter bandwagon, too. Apparently I had passed a crucial test, one far more important than simply demonstrating skill in crooked gambling.

I released Skip's wrist and he stood up straight, pulling down his apron. He put on a pair of glasses and studied my list with new interest. "I think . . ."—he pronounced it *t'ink*— ". . . that you and me were speaking different languages before."

He waggled his cigar to the corner of his mouth. "For instance, maybe what you call *glims* ain't what I call *glims.*"

"Well, let me t'ink. I've heard some people call them *shiners. Flicks* and *twinkles,* too. Those words ring any bells?" A glim was a concealed mirror that enabled the player to read the cards he was dealing.

Skip nodded and put a check mark on my list. He tapped his pencil down the column and made more marks. "Well, what do you know? Maybe you and me can do business, after all."

With his pencil behind his ear and his glasses drooping on the end of his nose, Skip wandered into the back room with my list. The man with the pistol took fresh aim at the bathing beauty.

Skip returned in ten minutes, carrying a box of Grape Lick-Pops—the Licorice-Filled Lollipop. He raised the lid long enough to show me that everything on my list was underneath the first two layers of lollipops.

Even though I couldn't afford to spend time haggling, I had to make it look good. I talked Skip into lowering his asking price twice before I finally nodded in agreement. When he asked me for the money, I couldn't resist showing off. I tugged back my sleeve and displayed my empty palm. With a snap of my fingers, a wad of bills filled my hand. I handed them to Skip and said, "That's the exact number of dollars. Count them if you want. And now for your change." I snapped my fingers several more times. With each snap, a coin materialized in midair, bounced on the counter, and rolled around before stopping in front of the dollar bills. Skip counted the money.

"Not bad," he said. "Uh, here." He pulled out a sheet of green perforated paper from the counter—saving stamps. "You can get a lot of neat stuff with these. Last week my wife got a toaster for only two books." He stuffed my money into his cigar box.

As I pocketed the stamps, I noticed that although Skip seemed impressed by my finger-flinging, his smile was lasting too long. His face almost had a pained look. I wondered what hot water my showing off had gotten me into this time when suddenly I heard the clacking of the lock on the main door behind me. Skip's chest heaved and he released a long hissing breath, his eyes clamping shut. When he opened them again, they were no longer dull and listless, instead they looked like smooth, polished rocks. He must have sent a secret signal—perhaps hitting a foot pedal while leaning forward to scoop up my money.

Shoving my box tightly up under my arm, I did my best to smile; but my lips felt as sticky and brittle as Lick-Pops. My feet made flat echoes on the concrete floor and it seemed to take forever to reach the door. I jiggered the knob, but it wouldn't turn. I set my box of lollipops on the table where the doorman had been playing solitaire. The doorman slid back his folding chair with a screeing sound like long fingernails on cold slate. He slowly undid the button on his blazer.

Skip untied his apron, stubbed out his cigar, and began edging toward me. He was flanked on either side by two back-room employees who had obviously been hired not only to toss boxes onto high shelves but to toss bulky packages into rivers at night. They were both opening and closing their fists, warming up the muscles they had lovingly developed during long barbell sessions. As he and his friends stepped nearer, Skip spoke soothingly.

"How about telling us your real name, son."

"What's up, Skip? All of a sudden my money's no good? A little late for a credit check, isn't it?"

"No credit check, son. We don't do business that way." He looked to his sides to make sure his partners were level with him.

"So what's the problem?"

"I ran another kind of check on you. How about telling me again who sent you here?"

I felt like a student taking a pop quiz on material I hadn't read. Thinking I'd never need them again, I had mentally discarded all the names the bartender had given me. I tried to retrieve them, but they were all jumbled together into one giant anagram.

Trying to laugh off the threat, I spoke to Skip with the savvy of a streetwise man with nothing to lose. Truth was, the streets of my childhood neighborhood had been clean and quiet and lined with shade trees . . . a sharp contrast to the gutted buildings and abandoned cars surrounding Candyland. On top of that, I *did* have a great deal to lose: I had worked too long and hard for the lollipop box I'd just bought. There wasn't time to replace it.

Besides, grape was my favorite flavor.

I shoved my hands into my pockets and felt the reassuring chill of steel—the same steel that had saved me in many scrapes. In my other pocket, my third and fourth fingers curled around two plastic capsules, drawing them into what magicians call a finger palm.

"What was that first name you mentioned?" Skip asked.

The name popped into my head and I tossed it out like a hunk of meat to the lions. "Swanson. Moe Swanson."

I shot a glance behind me. I recognized the dead-bolt lock on the door as one of the few dozen types I was proficient with. I withdrew my hands from my pockets and showed them empty. Of course they weren't.

Skip and his boys were proud of graduating from the school of hard knocks, but I had a special degree, too—from a school whose only teacher was a three-way mirror in my bedroom. I had also done postgrad work in smoky nightclubs where my act was nothing more than a segue between the nightly fistfights and the first-string team of strippers.

I took a step backward and the doorknob rudely jabbed my lower back. Gesturing with my right hand—pivoting the capsules into a back palm to keep them hidden—I told Skip to give Swanson a call.

The lines on his pudgy face rearranged themselves into a smug grin. "Oh, I already did that. And guess what Swanson said?"

I already had an idea of what he said. I was more concerned with the chatters and ticks of the metal I was working on behind me.

"Swanson told me about a smooth-looking guy who hung around his joint all afternoon, making small talk and doing card tricks for the boys at the pool tables. Every once in a while, this guy with the tricks would slip in a few questions about wanting to buy hot goods. When anyone raised an eyebrow, he'd buy a round of drinks and start back in with his tricks."

My fingertips felt the next-to-the-last tumbler give way.

Skip said, "Look, buddy, it's not that we don't enjoy your company. It's just that . . ."

The lock behind me emitted a familiar click, and the door glided open a quarter inch. I felt as though a pile of bricks had been lifted from my chest.

" . . . when a stranger buys that kind of merchandise, we got to be careful that . . ."

As Skip talked, I returned my lock picks to my pocket and picked up my lollipops. ". . . he's not some kind of—Jesus! He's got a gun!"

I spun around. *Who's* got a gun? The doorman beside me still had his piece holstered. The two gorillas on either side of Skip were also empty-handed. The man with the silencer had disassembled his iron and was slinking toward the back room, trying not to get caught in a fray that wasn't his business.

Then I realized whom Skip was talking about—me. *I* was the one who supposedly had a gun. But of course I wasn't armed. All I had was a box of lollipops in my left hand, and two capsules—one filled with ammonia and the other with hydrochloric acid—in my right.

With a synchronization developed only from plenty of time together in the trenches, the doorman and Skip's two henchmen dipped their hands into their coats. So that was their plan. They weren't sure if I was an undercover cop or a spy from an organized-crime family. Skip had been careful to speak clearly when calling out about my fictitious gun, just in case I was a cop wired for sound. They intended to search me, and if they found a bug, they'd confiscate my purchase and let me go. But if they found out that I wasn't from the police, I was going to end up in the river tonight.

I hooked my heel in the space between the door and jamb, saying, "Sorry, Skip. No action today. Your boys will just have to be content with hefting cases of Sugar Daddies and Almond Joys." I kicked sideways and the door creaked open. Sunshine spilled into the dank warehouse. For one crazy moment I thought that the fresh air and natural light would cause them all to shriek and run for cover, but they held their ground.

I said, "I wish I could stay and continue our discussion, but I've got a show tonight." I squeezed the two capsules together and cracked them. I flung them to the floor in front of Skip, and an opaque wall of smoke shot up between me and all my new friends.

While they coughed and sputtered and ducked and yelled, "Where the hell's the fire extinguisher?" I slipped through the doorway. Outside, I rushed behind the warehouse to the alley where my van was waiting.

For the next few blocks, my engine begged me to obey the speed limit. I ran stop signs at the quieter intersections, constantly checking my side mirrors to make sure I wasn't followed. After several minutes of sudden turns down narrow alleys, I pulled into the parking lot of a fast-food restaurant and opened my box of Lick-Pops. I peeled the wrapper off one of the lollipops and slipped it under my tongue, letting the tangy flavor relieve the dryness in my throat.

When my heartbeat had calmed down as much as it was going to, I examined the gimmicks I'd just bought. Each was meant to give me an edge at the card table. My final two purchases had been impulse buys: a miniature camera that looked like a bulky tie clasp and a nickel-plated two-shot derringer.

As I exited the lot, I reminded myself to replenish my supply of smoke capsules and to call the talent manager of the Mystic Isle to tell him I was taking the night off. As I wended my way along the side streets of Parrish—no longer worried about being tailed—I thought of the side streets that my professional career had taken during recent years. If I could come up with as smooth an exit for my regular act as I'd pulled off today at Candyland, I'd have no trouble getting back on TV again.

Waiting at a red light, I played with one of my new toys: a hold-out, designed to silently deliver cards from up my sleeve into my palm. Beeping horns from behind reminded me the light had turned green. Steering with one hand, I continued to monkey with the hold-out. It would take several hours of tedious practice to learn to use the equipment without detection.

However I had no choice. The life of Cate Fleming, my former assistant, depended on my expertise.

CHAPTER TWO

Fifty years ago the town of Parrish in the Pennsylvania Cat-
skills was home to three thriving anthracite mines and a modest
steel mill. But times turned sour, and the pits were sealed when
the coal became too expensive to mine. At about the same time,
the steel mill was absorbed by a conglomerate whose appetite
was bigger than its stomach. The new owner quickly resold the
mill to a Korean company that, in turn, decided it was more
economical to board up the plant then to modernize it. Parrish
never fully recovered from the blow, and much of the labor force
fled to greener pastures. A few fly-by-night garment factories
sprang up to exploit the unemployed workers who remained. The
employees there joked darkly about dashing to the bank each
week to cash their paychecks before they bounced.

Although only a few miles from several large mountain resorts, Parrish profited little from tourism. Among its few claims
to fame were the luxurious summer homes dotting its outskirts.
The houses were built a generation ago by several entertainers
who had leaped from the borscht circuit into prominence but
still loved the mountain air. Today, most of these houses were
still summer retreats, but were now owned by people with quite
varied backgrounds. The most notable summer resident was Lisa
South, the well-known gossip columnist and TV interviewer.

Parrish was also proud of the Mystic Isle, an all-magic nightclub that drew patrons mostly from the surrounding resorts. Six
years ago I'd have pompously recommended the Mystic Isle as
an ideal place for a budding magician to cut his teeth. Back then
I thought my days of playing clubs were behind me. Today I had
fourth billing at the Mystic Isle, beneath a comic contortionist
who told tasteless anatomical jokes, an aging balloon sculptor

who bragged incessantly about his 457 appearances on *Captain Kangaroo,* and a memory expert who suffered from melancholia. I tried not to remind myself that my only job offer beyond this engagement was to play a character called Grandpop at the grand opening of a chain of Mom and Pop's convenience stores. I was supposed to wear a baker's apron and perform magic while smoking a giant pipe. I told the public-relations director I'd think about it.

As for my job at the Mystic Isle, it had been embarrassingly easy to get tonight off. The talent manager had to consult his list of acts to remember who I was. I could have skipped out without calling him and he never would have noticed.

Six years can change a lot of things.

Six years ago I had just finished taping my first television special. Six years ago Cate Stanley had been my assistant, and I was contemplating asking her to become Mrs. Harry Colderwood. But I had never raised the subject, figuring there would always be plenty of time. In those days there seemed to be time for everything.

But soon after taping that show, my career—and, it seemed, my whole life—suddenly derailed. Although I managed to patch some of the pieces together, they never felt comfortable again. My special was canceled, and Cate's last name never became Colderwood. After she quit our act (claiming that I cared more about my magic equipment than about her) she pursued an acting career, with only lukewarm results. Apparently marriage became more attractive to her than the constant rejection of cattle-call auditions. She married a man named Phil Fleming, a physical-fitness buff who manufactured exercise equipment. I had seen her only once since our parting, when she helped me solve the murder of a clown found in a hotel safe.

A few days ago Cate surprised me with a phone call saying that she was a full-time actress again and that her marriage to Phil Fleming had been a mistake—an even bigger mistake than her years as my assistant. While waiting for her divorce to become final, she had taken a chorus line job in a revue at the Mount Pacifica Resort. She was emphatic—too emphatic—that her being in the same town as me was pure coincidence.

Cate reluctantly accepted my invitation to dinner, warning me not to expect much. Over cocktails, she declared that our date meant nothing more to her than a chance to confide in an old buddy. Her parting kiss was cool and impersonal, convincing me that I'd never hear from her again.

But Cate called me again this morning. And it wasn't for a date. Cate Fleming was the reason I was standing here tonight on this sidewalk in front of a store that specialized in aids to the sick and infirm. I checked the knot of my tie in the reflection of the store window and hoped for a breeze to chase away the oppressive August heat. My coat and tie felt as constraining as the straitjacket in my escape act, but I had to wear them in order to use the stuff I bought today at Candyland. I pulled up on my tie, but the jeweled tie pin—resembling a grotesquery from a South Seas tourist shop—made the tie sag again.

I peered through the window at a clock above a shelf of oxygen tanks. Five till eight. A car horn tapped rhythmically and I spun around, instinctively flattening myself against the shop door. I peeled myself away when I saw that the passing car was loaded with teenage boys who were paying their respects to two girls sauntering down the sidewalk. When the girls ignored them, the boys roared off in search of more promising streets.

I took one last look at myself in the glass door. I squeezed my elbow against my side and felt the click of the shutter release I had fastened to my rib cage with adhesive tape. I then slid my thumb along the serrated wheel on the side of my tie tack, advancing the film inside the miniature camera. I took a deep breath and the adhesive tape pulled at my skin.

My ribs weren't the only place I had taped. A few rings of tape around my ankle held in place the derringer I had bought. Though I had no intention of using it, it was comforting to know it was there, in case I got into a jam that a wave of my magic wand couldn't solve.

The clock inside the surgical fitters store (surely it was my imagination that its hands looked like tiny crutches) now said five past. As I kept an eye on the waning traffic, I scratched an itch underneath my taped ribs, accidentally exposing another frame of film. While I was winding the camera, a black limousine, glistening like a giant patent-leather shoe, lurched to a stop in front of the shop. Its front hubcap ground sickeningly against the curb. I tried to look inside the car, but the dark windows were like mirrors. The driver shifted into Park and laid heavily on the gas, causing the hood to vibrate and hitch clumsily from side to side.

The back door fell open, affording me a tantalizing view of a pair of long legs. The legs belonged to a blonde whose face had a fragile, pale cast. She uncrossed her legs and squirmed toward the center of the backseat, taking her time, aware that I was thoroughly enjoying the way her dress had crept upward. There was another pair of legs next to hers—a man's, clothed in rumpled corduroy. She tapped a slender finger on the seat beside her, inviting me inside. Her smile said that if that pair of corduroys weren't there, she'd be game for more than just sitting beside me.

I rested my hand on the roof and leaned inside.

"Are you folks by any chance on your way to, uh—"

"A poker game," the blonde said, her voice low and musical. "Are you coming or what? You're holding us up."

I shrugged and got in. When I closed the door, the driver—a man with a mustache and black hair so curly his hat didn't fit—got out and walked around the car. He wanted to make sure I was alone. After getting back in, he jerkily steered the car into traffic, amid the protests of horns and squealing tires behind us. The woman slid closer to me. Her hair was swept back on one side to reveal a two-inch-long diamond earring. The other side of her blond mane cascaded down over the front of her shoulder, partially covering the border of her strapless gown, just grazing the top of her breasts.

I tried to look out the window, but the dark glass prohibited me from distinguishing much more than the flash of car headlights. I leaned forward, trying to keep my bearings by looking through the windshield.

The blonde pressed her thigh to mine, but I kept sliding away until my elbow was jammed against the door. She had a hurt, quizzical expression, but I couldn't explain that I wasn't being antisocial. I simply didn't want her brushing against the gun taped to my ankle.

I leaned my head against the window and tried to steady myself by focusing my mind on the good times Cate and I had had together. But calm eluded me as one thought kept assailing me: if I failed tonight, all those good times would be locked forever in the past tense. With nothing more to add.

CHAPTER THREE

Although the limo was now moving at a safer speed, the woman beside me had apparently had enough of watching the driver struggle with the wheel. She briskly closed the velvety curtain separating the front and back seats, cutting off my view through the windshield. After a few minutes of peering out my side window, I gave up trying to make sense of the lights and shadows zipping past. I leaned back and feigned relaxation.

I tried making conversation, but my smallest small talk seemed too big for this crew. "My name's Harry," I said. The plush, coffinlike interior of the limousine seemed to swallow my words.

A few moments went by and the man in the corduroy trousers sighed and said, "I'm John. And this is Nicole. Pleased to meet you, I'm sure." He turned away, as though having completed a nasty duty.

John wore a navy blue insulated jacket with zippered pockets. Too warm for outside, it was perfect for the chilly air inside the car. Although his hands were youthful and pampered, with nails recently manicured, the shriveling at the corners of his eyes and mouth was that of a man nearing sixty. Thick veins pulsed close to the surface of his temples. His beak of a nose was short and barely seemed to support his thin-framed eyeglasses. His dull gray hair—with only a few patches of brown remaining—was combed back on the sides, tucked carelessly behind his ears. His hands folded, John stared straight ahead through hooded eyes. The key to beating John at the card table would not be through his emotions. He looked as unflappable as a computer terminal.

Not knowing how long we'd be, I had come prepared. I pulled out one of two packs of cigarettes from my pocket. I offered a cigarette to John and Nicole, but they shook their heads no. My

14

match had just settled down to a steady flame, ready to touch the end of my cigarette, when the whiny electronic voice of the driver came over an overhead speaker: "Sorry, sir. You can't smoke in here."

Nicole's breath warmed my fingers as she blew out my match. She chuckled derisively. "Serves you right. It's your business if you want to poison yourself, but why take the rest of us with you?"

I sighed and then smiled. "People like you make self-destruction such a lonely task."

I amused myself with a mental image of myself leaning across the card table and taking in all of Nicole's chips. Instead of dismissing the image, I let it unfold, savoring the victory. In my mind, I saw Nicole playing long after she was broke. She started betting her jewelry and moved on to throwing articles of clothing into the pot . . . until she had to cross her arms to hide her nakedness. When I turned over my final winning hand, she whistled admiringly and said, *"Now that's card playing."* The limo jounced to a halt at an intersection, shattering my fantasy.

I dropped my extinguished match into the door ashtray and twisted the cigarette back into the pack. When I returned the pack to my pocket, my fingers settled on another box—slimmer, heavier, and more reassuring than my smokes. A deck of red Aviators—poker size. I took them out, flipped open the lid, and dumped them out. With my cards securely in hand, I felt as though a potent muscle relaxant had just kicked in.

The cards were limp and pliable, their formerly white borders a dingy brown. I squared the deck and did a sloppy dovetail shuffle, the kind a Sunday bridge player might do.

I clumsily dealt the cards on my lap, watching for any reaction from Nicole and John. Nicole was busily studying her scarlet fingernails while John slouched farther down in his seat. He popped a piece of candy in his mouth, and soon the whole car smelled of raspberry, an odor the driver apparently didn't mind.

After dealing out the whole deck, I gathered them up and started again. My mind returned to Cate's phone call this morning. For the first time I could think about it without my stomach turning to lead:

"Harry, it's Cate," she had said. Her words were sluggish and I thought there was a trace of shame in her voice. "Someone's . . . someone's got me."

It was six A.M. and I was trying to clear my head of the dream world I'd awakened from. Was Cate really on the phone or was she a part of my dream? I wasn't sure yet. *"Who's* got you?"

"I don't know. I can't see his face. He forced his way into my dressing room last night."

"Where are you?"

Her voice faded away and I missed the next words. Then: "—and I just don't know. He says he'll kill me. And I believe him."

"Did he—?"

"No, he hasn't harmed me. Yet. But I've been tied up and blindfolded all night."

I next heard Cate's muffled voice interrupted by a man's. Then she said, "You must follow his instructions if you want to see me alive again. You'll find an envelope at the hotel desk." She was obviously reading this part now. It was almost laughable to hear Cate Fleming, graduate of the American Academy of Dramatic Arts, reading lines as woodenly as a student auditioning for the class play. Hell, I thought, the Cate Fleming I know would have delivered those lines perfectly, achieving precisely the urgency the kidnapper wanted.

"Harry, I l—" The line went dead and I was listening to dial tone.

Clad in my robe and slippers, I rode the elevator to the hotel lobby. If anyone stared or snickered, I didn't notice. All I remembered was sitting on a leather couch beside a ridiculous artificial palm tree, reading and rereading the contents of the envelope the desk clerk handed me. The note was printed in florid, medieval letters on green stationery so thick that the creases in it left ugly scars. I rubbed my finger across the letters and didn't feel the indentations of metal typewriter hammers. The son of a bitch had printed the note on a daisy-wheel printer. Maybe even composed it on a word processor.

The note, written in the same high style as a government proclamation, contained detailed instructions. First, I was warned against telling the police—or anyone else—about the kidnapping. I was to go to the corner of East End Avenue and Kersey Street, where a driver would take me to a poker game. The note clearly stipulated that I *must* walk away the big winner from the game if I wanted to see Cate again. It said I didn't have to bring any cash with me. I would later be given instructions on where to drop off my winnings.

But the words that nagged at me the most weren't in the note. They were the ones uttered by Cate before the line was disconnected: *"I l—"*. All day, words starting with *l* tumbled through my mind. I became a walking thesaurus. Even now, sitting in this limo, dealing out cards in an inane game of solitaire whose rules I was making up as I went along, *l*-words continued to flow. But there was one I kept avoiding.

I looked at Nicole and said. "Name a word beginning with *l*."

"Let me see. How about *love?*"

I allowed myself a hint of a smile. "That's what I thought you'd say."

A minty odor was in the air now. John had switched from candy to breath mints. I gathered up my cards, noting that my all-thumbs style of card handling didn't draw a second glance from either of them. Good.

My shuffling and dealing was anything but aimless. It was a run-through of the sleights I would use tonight to wipe out my opponents: bottom deals, second deals, invisible cuts, and false shuffles.

Hand me any deck of cards and I can ordinarily stack it in thirty seconds. Anyone skilled in basic card magic could do the same. But conditions at a poker table are a hundred times more severe than when performing simple card magic. And the penalty for error is a hell of a lot stiffer. When I flub a trick in my magic show, the worst that can happen is a few boos and catcalls.

But tonight was no magic show. If I got caught with my sleight of hand in the cookie jar, I could end up with a bullet between my innocent brown eyes. As John reached in his jacket for another mint, I saw a metallic flash that definitely was not from the aluminum on his candy wrap. It was from the .45-caliber semiautomatic Colt in his shoulder holster.

Finger-flinging alone would not hold me in good stead tonight. Because of the severe conditions, I needed extra ammunition. That's why I'd taken that shopping trip to Candyland—Parrish's friendly purveyor of wholesale candy, illicit firearms, hot goods, and gimmicked gambling paraphernalia.

I continued practicing my card moves until the limo came to its final stop. Sliding the cards into their box and folding over the lid, I felt a pang in my stomach, as though I'd just been separated from friends in a strange, hostile town.

The driver said over the speaker: "Last stop and good luck, folks. Hope you all come home winners."

Go to hell, I thought. Nobody but me can win tonight. Otherwise Cate will be the big loser.

CHAPTER FOUR

We were standing inside a one-car garage barely large enough for the limousine. Careless pyramids of boxes and paint cans crowded the walls. The driver remained at the wheel, the car engine ticking and tapping as it started to cool down. The three of us crossed and uncrossed our arms uneasily, waiting to see who would move first. John took the lead and walked to a white door at the side of the garage. Putting his face to the glass, he said, "I see a light. Someone must already be down there."

He clicked open the door and disappeared into the dark. After a few seconds, Nicole and I followed and found ourselves in a shadowy walkway. As we edged along, I heard the whir of the electric garage door. The limo rumbled to life again, and I looked back to see its headlights throwing a blanket of light on a wall full of ladders, tools, and coiled wire. John halted suddenly and the three of us accordioned into one another. I trod on the back of Nicole's pumps as she jerked to the side to avoid squashing John.

"For crissakes," he said. "I hope I never go on a hike with you two."

I heard a thonk as John worked the latch of another door, followed by the gentle singing of door hinges. When we emerged from the passageway, I saw that the glow was coming from the bottom of a carpeted stairway. I could smell a combination of beer and oily snack food.

A man's voice called from below, sounding muffled. "John? Nicole?"

"Yeah," Nicole said, elbowing past us.

The garage door chattered closed, deadening the engine sound

19

of the limo, now parked outside. In a few seconds, the car drove off. Starting down the stairway, John said, "Miles, is that you?"

As I descended the steps, I heard clinking glasses and the rustle of Nicole's tafetta dress. From the quick smacking sounds that followed, I figured she was giving the guy named Miles a hug and kiss.

The staircase led into a spacious game room illuminated by fluorescent lights hidden above a ceiling of grainy plastic squares. The carpet was so thick that walking across it too fast meant risking a twisted ankle. Dominating the center of the room was a round table covered with felt, the color and texture of a golf green. Five naugahyde captain's chairs encircled it. On top of the table lay a brushed suede attaché case. At the far end of the room stood a Gold Crown pool table with a rack of balls that reflected the light like cut glass. A row of pool cues with Elk Master tips lined the side wall. On the opposite wall hung a dart board that at first appeared unused. When I got closer, I saw that the bull's-eye was riddled with tiny holes. Someone here certainly took his games seriously.

I assumed that the fleshy man standing in the corner was Miles. He moved to the sofa and let his big frame collapse onto it. He began flipping through a carved wooden case packed with compact discs, every so often plucking one out and dropping it on his lap. In his mid-forties, Miles wore clothes that would look trendy on someone half his age: a leather vest, trousers with broad stripes of fuchsia and white, and running shoes so expensive that the people who wore them were usually nonathletic. He wore glasses with frames that looked like sticks of glass candy. His hair was a carefully tended brush cut; however, he sported the ragged beginnings of a beard.

"So your name is Miles?"

His hand popped up at me like a dog's paw at the command of *shake*. His handshake had no grip. "Yep, that's my handle, at least when we're playing cards."

The determined set of his jaw told me that no amount of prodding would get him to reveal his real name.

"My turn to play host tonight, Miles," Nicole said. "What are you having?"

"A Genny Light will do."

"I'd better see if that's on stock." She went into the kitchen and opened the fridge. It was filled with cans, bottles, meats, and cheeses. "Yeah, we got it." She opened the cupboard door above the microwave to reveal a three-deep selection of liquor bottles. She dumped out two grocery bags onto the counter and inspected the packages of pretzels, chips, and peanuts, filling bowls and setting out ice and glasses. Her manner was unhurried, as though the upcoming game didn't weigh upon her at all.

Miles was a different matter. While sorting through the collection of compact discs, his face bore the concentration of a diamond cutter splitting a once-in-a-lifetime stone. After making his selections, he stooped in front of the stereo cabinet and started tapping buttons, programming in the songs he wanted to hear. He pressed a wrong sequence of buttons and groaned, then jabbed at them harder.

"I'm not used to this machine yet," he said. "A few more weeks and I'll get the hang of it." He stood up and paced in front of the sofa, waiting for the music to begin. When the first strains of a blues guitar oozed from the speakers, he slouched down on the sofa. Closing his eyes, he drummed his fingers on his thighs and tapped his feet.

I ventured out into the kitchenette. "What's your pleasure?" Nicole asked.

My mouth moistened at the sight of the beer she had poured for Miles, but I said, "How about coffee?"

"I don't know. The others aren't coffee drinkers. But there might be some in the bottom cupboard."

I opened the door. "You'd better believe there's coffee here. Four styles of roast, including hazelnut and Swiss mocha." I measured out enough of a hearty-smelling Colombian grind to make four cups, then threw in an extra scoop. As I watched the brown liquid trickle into the glass coffeepot, I said, "How often do you play here, Nicole?"

She fielded my question like a top-notch salesman handling a complaint, zinging it back with plenty of topspin: "Often enough to know the rule against discussing personal business. I—"

She stopped when she realized that I was staring at her bare shoulders and the smooth white tops of her breasts. She didn't turn away, but stood there motionless for several seconds, enjoying my fascination. Then she picked up her tall drink. With the pleasure of a reader savoring a good book, she slowly raised her glass of Collins and downed it in two long swallows. Perhaps this was supposed to give me a chance to gracefully turn my eyes elsewhere, but I continued to stare. Something about her pride in her body—her confidence that men found her magnetic—kept me from feeling awkward. Her full lips glistening from her drink, she said, "Shall we join the others?" I followed her out into the game room, aware of how easily her warmth and beauty had almost made me lose sight of my purpose here tonight.

John was seated at the table, counting stacks of poker chips from the attaché case. From two rows of sealed decks, he pulled out a pack of blue Bicycles and tossed it to the center of the table. He took out a plastic-tipped cigar and clenched it at an angle in his yellow teeth, unlit.

The overhead light made John's face appear even more drawn. Dark pouches had found a home under his eyes. When he moved his head, loose skin swung under his chin like the folds of a curtain in a breeze. Nicole asked John if he was hungry and he shook his head.

"Where's old Les?" John asked. "In the can again?"

As though in answer, a nearby toilet flushed, followed by the sound of running water. The sound grew louder as the door on the other side of the game room opened, and a fit-looking man in his late sixties walked out. He wore a white shirt and gray tie, and carried a black suit jacket which he slipped on. A gray silk handkerchief protruded from the breast pocket. A craggy-faced man, Les wore his red hair in a short, neat style. He headed for the table with the briskness of a man late for an appointment. Les curtly acknowledged each of the players with a nod; but when he laid eyes on me, his face warmed. "What have we here?" he said. "New blood? How about sitting beside me? Might bring me some luck for a change." He patted the chair beside him, and I walked over and sat down.

As the others took their places around the table, Nicole set a glass in front of Les that was filled with shaved ice and a red liquid that smelled more fruity than alcoholic. He stirred it, took a sip, and savored the flavor before taking another.

Miles planted himself near a basket of potato chips and immediately dug in, crunching two and three chips at a time. His hand only strayed from the basket once, to wipe his fingers on his trousers. When the basket was empty, he washed everything down with a long pull from his mug of beer. He thunked it down mightily on the table, signaling that not only was he ready to play, he was ready to pick us clean—to the bone.

John began calling out our names and shoving stacks of chips across the table. In what he thought was a confidential voice, Les gave me a rundown of the value of each chip. I reached for my wallet, pretending I wanted to pay for my chips, but John held up his hand, saying that all tabs would be settled at the end of the night. Good, I thought. Thus far, everything outlined in the ransom note was coming to pass. After my visit to the candy warehouse, I didn't have enough in my wallet to cover even the cheapest chip. I drained the last of my coffee and noted that my nerves were already feeding off the caffeine and felt razor-sharp. I slid the cup aside, deciding not to drink anything else tonight. I wanted to be as clear-headed as possible.

As I settled back in my chair, I lightly patted my pants and coat pockets, checking on my hidden apparatus. Everything was in position: a packet of stripped cards (trimmed so I could easily locate them after adding them to the deck), a vial of daub for secretly marking cards, a deck of blisters (cards marked with bumps), a bug clip for hiding cards under the table, two sets of glims, and a hold-out fastened up my coat sleeve. The only piece of equipment I didn't check was the derringer under my sock— brute modern magic in case the sorcerer's old-fashioned spells failed tonight.

John ripped away the cellophane from the deck and did a meticulous riffle shuffle, handling the cards as if he were conducting a religious ritual. Nicole stared eagerly at the cards, as if the curtain were rising on a play she knew she would love. As Les lowered his glass from his lips, I saw a gleaming in his eyes, an absolute hunger to win. Although Miles was trying to maintain a cool facade, his constant rearranging of his chips gave him away. He rubbed his lower lip nervously against the jagged edges of his front teeth.

After squaring the deck, John paused and took note of the mild tremor in his hands. This minor loss of control didn't seem to worry him. In fact, he seemed to thrive on it. He smartly slapped down the cards in front of me. Trying not to overdo my clumsiness, I performed a single cut and passed the deck back to John, letting him square it. "Five-card draw," he announced and began flicking cards to each of us.

I knew my first card was the King of Hearts before I even peeked at it. When cutting the deck, I had crimped the corner of the King of Hearts and left it at the bottom of the deck. But

John had other plans for it and made sure it ended up in front of me. My respect for him increased. Starting with the very first hand, John was dealing off the bottom. With flawless technique.

As he continued to deal, my hand crept over to my tie clasp. I slowly swiveled my seat back and forth, snapping pictures of everyone.

The game had begun.

CHAPTER FIVE

9:10 P.M.

At the start of the evening, my stacks of chips had looked like the Manhattan skyline. They now resembled a row of town houses in Shamokin. I had played a conservative game, folding each hand early, allowing the others to shoot it out among themselves. This gave me a chance to study everyone's weaknesses.

Thus far, Miles was deservedly the big winner. Although he mostly played the percentages, he bluffed often enough to keep the others from automatically folding when he began to bet big. Although the other three players were easy prey for Miles, he still wasn't satisfied. He eyed my chips greedily, annoyed that they weren't flowing into his coffer fast enough.

As I folded my latest hand—a pair of threes—I thought about the flaws of the other players. Nicole was hurt by her very exuberance for the game. She consistently telegraphed the value of her hand, blinking too much at good hands and puckering her lips to the side when she was holding garbage.

John had the most poker savvy of the four, but his playing reminded me of a '62 Chevy I once owned. That car would run fine until the speedometer edged over seventy-five. Then it would scream and shimmy as if the engine was about to rip through the hood. That's the way John played poker: safe and sane until he attempted a crucial move, and then his composure crumbled. A few times he became so lost in sweaty indecision that we had to remind him it was his turn to bet. Once, while agonizing over his cards, he even let his hand dip forward, flashing to everyone the straight he was holding.

But Les was the oddest of all. He put up a good show, laughing when he won and cursing when the cards didn't go his way. But I wondered just how much he wanted to win. During one hand, I knew that he needed a King to make a full house. Since it was my deal, I made sure he drew the necessary card. Upon receiving the King, his face fell and his jaw clenched. He slid his cards together and for a moment I thought he was going to fold. Although he stayed in and won the hand, his delight over the victory seemed forced.

After another hour of gradual losing, I decided it was time to make my move—to make Miles wonder what the hell hit him.

9:50 P.M.

The tide had begun to turn in my favor and Miles was starting to worry. He shielded his cards with his pawlike hands, as though suspecting I could see through them. But his efforts were futile—I knew what his cards were *before* they were dealt. Whenever it was my deal, I manipulated the cards I wanted to the top and dealt them to myself. Sometimes I palmed them off and executed a ''brush off''—passing my hand over facedown cards and switching them. Other times I relied on extra cards attached to the bug clip I had stuck under the table. The trick was to avoid adding cards to my hand that the others were already holding— some gamblers have a pet peeve about decks with more than fifty-two cards.

''What the hell—?'' Nicole said with a chuckle as she spread the cards that Les had just dealt her. For a second, I feared there were too many aces in her hand. I sweated it out until the end of the hand, when she revealed that one of my savings stamps from the candy warehouse was stuck to her Jack of Hearts. It must have been floating around in my pants pocket, damp from my perspiration.

Miles, Les, and John saw no humor in the stray stamp, but didn't raise a fuss over it. Perhaps one of them thought that the stamp had come from *his* pocket.

Tension got the best of me and I reached for my pack of cigarettes. But Nicole gave me a warning shake of her head and I put them away. No use breaking *all* the rules of the game tonight.

I checked my palm and made sure that no more stamps were stuck to it. Then I shuffled the cards and dealt myself three Queens.

11:00

Miles was reveling in what he thought was certain victory. The pot was a rainbow of colored plastic and he couldn't wait to rake it into his fold. My own supply of chips was down to a handful. Miles scratched his ear and hummed along with the music on the stereo, trying to make us think that his hand was junk. I knew he was holding a Jack-high straight.

When it came time to read 'em, Miles didn't weep, but he did raise an accusing finger at me when he saw that I also held a straight—*King*-high. Red in the face, he opened his mouth to object, but stopped when he realized he had nothing concrete to back up his suspicions. So far—except for the roving stamp—my moves had all been clean.

"Yes?" I said, staring at his raised finger. His finger dropped and his mouth closed.

"Nothing," he said. "My deal." I passed him the deck and captured the chips in the center of the table with a sweep of my arm.

"If you'll excuse me," I said, "I think I'd like to sit out a few hands."

As I headed for the stairway, Les called out, "Wrong way, Harry. The bathroom's through that door."

"Oh, yeah. Right." I had hoped to tour the house, but now I had to confine my exploration to the powder room.

The bathroom was sparsely decorated with functional white porcelain and simple chrome fixtures. It was cheerless, compared to the game room. The only window in the room was made of frosted glass, impossible to see through. I unlocked the window and raised it, making hardly a sound. Outside I could see a steep grassy embankment and could hear occasional nearby traffic. I had crawled halfway out the window when there was a knock at the door.

"Hey, Harry. Are you in this hand?" It was Miles.

"Yeah. I'll be out in a minute."

Pulling my leg inside, I lowered the window and fished in my pocket until I found another of the trading stamps from Candyland. I placed it facedown on top of the window frame—above eye level—and then drenched a wad of toilet paper in the sink. Putting one foot on the sill, I pulled myself up and wet down the wood directly above the window frame with the toilet paper.

Returning to the game room, I saw that John had switched to red-backed Aviator cards. Fine, I thought. That was the brand I had loaded into my hold-out—the mechanical device hidden up my sleeve. With a hold-out, I could change an entire hand of cards, seemingly without moving a finger.

Resuming my seat, I realized that they had suspended play while I was gone. They didn't want each other's chips anymore. They wanted mine.

12:15 A.M.

Miles drank from his mug, barely noticing that his beer was now all foam. He squinted at his cards and tried to appear calm, attempting to smooth out the deep lines in his face. Perspiration trickled down his beard, collected into big drops at the point of his chin, and fell to the table. The splats sounded like the tocking of a clock. After mumbling, "Time to go for it," he shoved forward his castles of chips. The others sat up straight, wearing amused expressions that were about to break into broad smiles. They were hoping that tonight would be different, that Miles would not be going home with their money.

After I matched his bet, Miles slipped his fingers under his cards, ready to reveal his hand. But I pointed a finger at the heap of chips in the pot and said, "Again."

"Hey, what more do you want?" Miles said. "I've bet everything I have."

I looked to John, who was already nodding his assent for additional financing. He took out a notepad to figure the amounts of our new wagers and then counted out the necessary chips.

Miles hesitated for only a second and then waved his finger at the stacks of chips that John had counted out, doubling the pot. After licking his lips, he flipped his cards faceup.

The sight of his full house hit me like a sledgehammer to the forehead. I no longer heard the music on the stereo or the quiet chitchat of the other players. Time froze as my mind raced to figure out what had happened. I had intended his hand to be a ten-high full house, not Queen-high. Where the hell did I go wrong? I looked for the crimped ten and saw that the only card in his hand with a crimped corner was a Queen. I realized that I had forgotten to uncrimp the Queen whose corner I had bent during my last deal. Sure enough, I saw that the deck in front of me was raised up a fraction in the center where the crimped ten now resided. My eyes burned with sweat and sudden tears at the thought that a lousy misdealt full house would cause Cate's death. Unless . . .

As my right hand reached to turn over my cards, my elbow bumped my coffee cup. Les's hand shot out to steady it. My left hand then took over the duty of spreading my cards. I triggered the hold-out inside my sleeve and felt a reassuring tickle as the metal rod glided out and—under the cover of my palm—neatly deposited five new cards into my right hand. I picked up my stack of cards from the table and slapped them into my right hand, making a total of ten cards. I spread out the new cards, keeping the five old ones palmed. Voila. An instant straight flush. It was Miles's turn to be hit by the sledgehammer.

Turning several shades paler, he sank in his chair and closed his eyes. After letting himself bleed internally for a few moments, his eyes flew open and he managed to work up a weak smile. Trying to play the part of the cheerful loser, he reached in his vest and pulled out a yellow envelope. Without even venturing a glance at me, he asked John what the total damages were. When John told him, Miles looked glassy-eyed at his envelope, unwilling just yet to settle his tab. As the tension around the table dissipated, I again became aware of everyone's breathing and squirming, of the R & B music on the CD player. John was now staring vacantly at the pile of chips in front of me. Something inside him seemed to have collapsed, like a brittle, dead flower.

When John finally snapped out of his funk, he took out a huge wallet connected by a chain to his belt and began counting out the money he had lost. Les and Nicole were next, leaving Miles to settle up. Seemingly unfazed by her losses, Nicole was quickly on her feet, on her way to mix one last drink. Miles removed the bills from his envelope one by one, as though each weighed a pound. Occasionally he made snuffling sounds and had to stop and wipe his nose with the side of his hand.

Les took Miles's and my cards and arranged them in two neat rows in front of him. I hoped he didn't notice the little curl in the corner of the Queen. "Now *that's* how you play poker," he said. "Ever think of charging for lessons? You could make a mint."

I laughed. "Three men taught me everything I know about

cards. Two of them are now dead from gunshot wounds, and the third is due for parole at the turn of the century.''

Les smiled and held up his hand in a no-thanks gesture, deciding those kind of poker lessons were too expensive. He pushed himself to his feet and hobbled to the bathroom, working the kinks out of his back and legs as he went.

I looked at the hill of money in front of me and figured the kidnapper would never miss the few extra hundred I would hold back to celebrate Cate's safe return in style.

12:50

While washing my hands in the bathroom, I felt a breeze. The window had been opened less than an inch. I felt along the top of the window frame for the savings stamp. It was gone. I laid the side of my head against the window and looked up. The stamp was stuck to the wood above the window. I ran my hand along the sill and it felt gritty. So, I thought, one of the poker players had taken a trip outside during the game. I looked at my watch and tried to recall the comings and goings of everyone between 11:10—the time I had first used the bathroom—and now. I remembered that each of them had paid one visit to the bathroom during that time period, and that they were all present during the last half hour of play, during my showdown with Miles.

As I left the bathroom, I listened to the music on the stereo. Still the blues. How fitting.

CHAPTER SIX

The kidnapper had left little to chance. Even if I'd wanted to, it would have been impossible for me to stick around to spy on his retrieval of the ransom money. The limousine dropped me off at the same corner where it had picked me up. A card under the welcome mat in the doorway of the surgical fitter's shop informed me that the drop-off site would be the base of the wildcat statue that was the mascot of the local high school. The message said I had to be in my room at the Spears Hotel by 1:30 A.M. to receive a phone call telling me where to find Cate. I looked at my watch. I'd have to break speed limits to make it back to my room in time.

I didn't waste time dreaming up a scheme to snare the kidnapper. I could never live with myself knowing that my unwillingness to play the duped magician had harmed Cate in any way. I wanted her back safe and whole. So I followed my orders implicitly.

It took seven minutes—and one year off the life of the tires of my van—to make it to the high school campus. I got out and walked toward the middle of the mall where the wildcat stood guard in the moonlight. The air was still and I heard the distant bell of a church clock that was several minutes slow. As I got closer, I saw that the savage glare on the face of the big stone cat had been nullified by the red and yellow paint of vandals. After shoving the knotted white plastic bag into the shadows beneath the hindquarters of the wildcat, I headed for the street. I stayed alert for movement from the dark school buildings that bordered the campus on three sides. I didn't think that the kidnapper would be dumb enough to claim his booty before I left, but I was antsy that some teenagers on a late-night prowl might accidently stumble upon the treasure under the cat. I also didn't want a passing cop to get the notion that I was a spray-paint prankster back for more fun.

Back in my van, I waited to catch my breath, looking back at the sculpture in the distance. Darkness dulled the brightest colors of the spray paint and seemed to restore power and dignity to the cat. Looking at my reflection in the rearview mirror, I lit a cigarette and wished I could say the same about myself. I drove for a few blocks before stopping to chuck the derringer down a corner sewer grate. Even though the gun hadn't weighed much, I felt a hundred pounds lighter.

Back in my room, I fired up another cigarette. I had been chain-smoking ever since leaving the sterile backseat of the limousine. I remembered how, on the drive back, Nicole said little, her eyes closing for increasingly longer periods. John had huddled in the corner, his head turned away, ranting to himself about not playing better. He resisted my attempts at conversation. His coldness seemed only partly due to the money he had lost and for a while I thought maybe he knew I had cheated. I feared he might pull his gun and demand a split of my take. But he kept quiet, perhaps figuring I'd expose his own crooked—though in-effective—ways. Besides the bottom deal, John had attempted a few other cheating moves, all to little advantage. Perhaps my play had actually heartened him, by proving that devious methods actually can work.

I was now sitting on my bed in my hotel room, back against the headboard, looking down at the three one-hundred-dollar bills on my lap . . . all that remained of tonight's winnings. I thought of the $97,000 stuffed in the plastic bag I had left in the custody of the wildcat; of how I could have paid the past-due storage bills on the illusions from my old stage act, which were now gathering dust in a warehouse out on the Coast. I thought of the new tricks I could have bought to update my show.

I briefly entertained the notion of driving to Philadelphia next weekend, hanging out at a convention hotel and assembling a card game with businessmen who were hot for action. A few weekends like that and I could outfit myself with a spanking new touring show. But once I did that, I could never think of myself as a magician again. I would have become the enemy.

After staring at the silent phone for a few minutes, I turned on the TV and performed the ritual of every person living on the road: the endless twisting of the channel selector, searching for something that held my attention for more than thirty seconds. I sometimes fantasized that turning the dial harder would somehow force intelligence and entertainment into the tube, but it never worked. I finally settled on a talk show that had a young magician on the panel. The magician was giving his opinions on the Middle East crisis and the hottest new movies. Five minutes later—and still no magic—the host asked the magician to move to the show's kitchen setting to demonstrate his favorite pancake recipe. I switched channels.

Fifteen minutes till two and the phone refused to ring.

On Channel Nine I watched a rebroadcast of a hockey game. After several seconds, I still couldn't find the puck in the midst of all the flying sticks and fists. I clicked over to a boxing match where two lethargic fighters in baggy trunks would have done well to switch to Channel Nine to pick up some fighting tips from the hockey players.

At 1:50 I turned down the sound on the television and turned on the radio. The announcer was plodding through the newscast, mispronouncing the multisyllabic places in the world where the latest bullets had been fired.

At 2:00 the phone rang, causing a dull pain to radiate from the center of my chest. When it rang a second time, I flicked off the radio, leaving the TV on. The silent prizefighters were now standing toe to toe, unable to deck each other. The referee was sweating more than they were.

"Hello."

I heard the buzz of several men talking in the background blending with the ringing of phones and someone's sporadic typing. I spoke again and the background noise grew fuzzy as the caller covered the phone with his hand. Faintly, a man's voice said, "He answered." There was a clunking noise as the phone was passed to another person.

"Harry?"

It was Cate.

"Are you all right?"

She paused, as though considering her answer. I waited, making a silent vow of revenge. Then she answered, "I'm fine. I guess."

Air escaped from my lungs in a gush, and the pain in my chest subsided. "Where are you? I'll be right over."

Cate said something unintelligible to someone else. Through her voice I heard several voices shouting curses. Except for the typewriters, it sounded like a barroom.

"For crissakes, are you okay? Did the kidnapper let you go?"

The cursing subsided and I heard the sound of slapping flesh and furniture clunking. A drunken voice kept saying over and over, "Hey . . . hey . . . hey . . ."

"Yeah, Harry, the kidnapper let me go. But I'm sure as hell not free."

I looked down at the hundred-dollar bills. They had somehow folded themselves into a single tight packet. Good trick, I thought. How did I do it?

"Then where . . . ?" I asked.

"I'm at the Parrish police station. I'm under arrest. They—" The drunk started blubbering and I couldn't understand what Cate said next.

"What did you say??"

"I said, the police think I killed Lisa South."

"The gossip columnist? How the—"

A man with a vanilla-smooth voice cut short our conversation. He identified himself as Sergeant Gibson. Since he seemed to dislike first names, I told him my name was Mr. Colderwood. I tried to reason with him, stating it was all a mistake, that Cate could never kill anyone.

I told him I was coming down to straighten everything out, but he told me that unless I was her attorney, I'd have to wait until nine tomorrow morning to see her. He hung up without giving Cate a chance to say good-bye.

Putting the phone back on the hook, I turned up the TV and switched back to the young magician on the talk show. He was wearing a frilly apron covered with pancake flour, but at least the son of a bitch was finally doing magic. I had learned the trick he was performing when I was nine years old. It depended upon a double-faced Ace of Spades and cost thirty-nine cents at any magic shop. He nearly flubbed it, briefly flashing the duplicate side of the Ace. Nevertheless, the audience rewarded him with polite applause. God help him if his former girlfriend ever got kidnapped and he had to use his magic skills to rescue her.

I kept the TV on since sleep was out of the question. I took out my deck of cards and played a fast game of solitaire. Then another . . . and another.

I won them all. That's because I cheated—something I was getting good at lately.

CHAPTER SEVEN

The morning fog had burned off the surrounding mountains and seemed to have rolled into the Anchor Coffee Shop. Cigarette smoke and the steam of coffee and soup hung in the air, laying a mist on the dirty front windows. Upon entering, I immediately noticed the uneasy coexistence of the townies and summer residents. They were sitting, respectively, at the counter and the tables. The townies were a boisterous lot. Passing the skimpy sections of the local paper among themselves, they wore an assortment of billed caps, T-shirts, and work trousers.

Those who sat at the tables were an average of fifteen to twenty years younger. Their reading heavily favored the *New York Times*, which they folded back into narrow sections to avoid dirtying their tennis and jogging clothes. Their designer tags were as proudly displayed as the monogrammed first names on the shirts of the guys at the counter. As the counter customers argued and jibed with each other about the upcoming Mets and Phillies game, those huddled in the booths talked in polite tones. Some looked up with annoyance at the whoops of laughter from the counter.

At the takeout counter, I ordered a large cup of black coffee and a giant muffin that had chocolate chips erupting all over it. I tore a half-inch section out of the lid of my cup so I could drink while driving. As the cashier counted my change, the conversation at the counter shifted to a topic that united the two factions of the coffee shop. Newspapers were lowered and both sides perked their ears as two men at the counter talked loudly.

"Did you hear about that South broad?"

"South of what?"

"No, no, that's her name. Lisa South. Don't you read?"

"Sorry. It doesn't ring a bell."

"She writes a newspaper column."

"Never heard of it. Does the *Parrish Tribune* carry it?"

"Nah, she's too big for the local paper. But I bet you've seen her TV specials. Interview stuff. Always talking to big-shot TV and movie stars. She was a real ace at making people cry. You could be a big macho actor or a linebacker for the Jets . . . it didn't matter. Sooner or later she'd get you talking about your last divorce or how crummy your parents treated you or how hard it was to quit drugs. Then watch out. Better get a hankie because—bamm!—the waterworks are going to start."

"Sounds like she should have been a shrink and made herself some real dough."

"Dough? Are you kidding? Didn't you ever see her house?"

"No."

"Hell, it's up in the Martin Hills section. I heard the place was loaded with art and jewelry. In fact that's why the police think she was offed. Some of that crap was missing." He unfurled his paper so his friend could read it. "See? They found her body this morning. A forty-five caliber slug in the back of the head."

His friend bit into his doughnut. Powdered sugar snowed down on the front-page photo of Lisa South. It was the same photo that always appeared above her column. Her small eyes looked fierce and she wore her red hair in a style so voluminous that much of it was cropped out of the picture. The photograph next to it was of a modest Spanish colonial home built against a hillside. The entrance to the house was obscured by a crowd of men on the front lawn, some in uniform and others in sports jackets. Many were taking notes. The man reading the article shook his head and spoke with his mouth full. "Weird. A summer home right here in Parrish and our paper's too cheap to print her column."

His friend spun around in his stool and spoke louder, for the benefit of those sitting at the booths and tables. "No, it's not weird at all. I think the *Tribune* was just showing good taste. After all, not everyone born here takes kindly to strangers invading the town, buying houses that cost more than I'll make in the next ten years—*before taxes*. Not everyone likes outsiders who live here a couple months a year and think that because they drive fancy German cars they can tell us how to run our town."

He glared at a man sitting in the booth in front of him. Wear-

ing fourteen-carat-gold-framed glasses with round lenses the size
of half-dollars, the man dabbed his lips with his napkin and
averted his eyes from the man at the counter. He asked the waitress for a blueberry Danish and an espresso.

"Now ain't that sweet," the man at the counter said. "It won't
be long before this place has wine on the menu."

The man at the table turned the page of his newspaper and
calmly resumed his reading, as if he were in the back corner of
a library. The man at the counter thumped the photo of Lisa
South and said, "Yep, maybe this will start a trend around here.
A new kind of Welcome Wagon."

His friend said, "Do the cops know who did the murder?"

"Sure. And don't think for one second it was one of *us*. According to the paper they arrested a showgirl from the Mount
Pacifica Resort. The name's Cate Fleming. Says here she's in her
mid-thirties. Getting a little long in the tooth to be called a 'girl,'
don't you think? The police figure she got ticked off at South for
busting up her marriage. It seems that South at one time had an
affair with this Fleming lady's husband."

"Hmmm, I don't see South's address here in the article. Do
you know where in Martin Hills she lives?"

"Sure. On Christopher Road."

"What do you say we take a drive past?"

"And just what the hell would we see?"

"Who knows? Maybe they haven't wheeled the body out yet."

The man shrugged and flattened his newspaper into a small
package and stuffed it into the front pocket of his checkered
Woolrich. He walked leisurely out of the shop, his friend at his
heels. A few seconds later, several other counter customers followed. I heard the words *ghouls* and *sickies* murmured several
times by those at the tables. But an uncomfortable hush gradually
descended over the coffee shop. It was broken by the shuffling
feet of the clean-cut, well-groomed customers, as they got up
table by table and filed out. The owner shook his head at the
dwindling clientele. Within a minute, I had my pick of any seat
in the shop.

For a moment, I considered buying a copy of the *Tribune*, but
decided that I'd rather hear Cate's version first. I took a drink of
coffee through the hole in the lid, wrapped my muffin in a napkin, and hurried outside in time to join the caravan of pickup

trucks, Chevies, and Mercedes—all wending their way toward the summer home of the late Lisa South.

Most of Christopher Road ran parallel to a steep grassy slope that was topped by thick timber. The houses on the slope were elevated far above the road level, while those on the other side were so low that their second stories were level with the pavement. Lisa South's home was located on the high side of Christopher and was easy to find. A simple white fence bordered the front yard and flowing down the center of the yard was a tiny stream that emptied into a reflecting pond, complete with a miniature water wheel—an unintentional parody of Parrish's industrial heritage. I slowed to a stop as I neared the driveway, noting that the scene at the front door was much the same as in the picture in the *Tribune*, except that some of the reporters were now sitting on the steps. When the cars behind me laid on their horns in protest, I continued along the winding road.

In need of directions, I drove for a few minutes and then pulled into a parking lot in front of a long warehouse with truck bays on the side. A clean white sign above the front door said Phoenix, Ltd. A section of railroad tracks, overgrown with scrub brush and weeds, ran along the side of the old building. Inside, a man wearing a black visor sat on a high stool behind a glass teller's window. He put down his clipboard and pen when he realized that I wasn't a truck driver. I remarked upon how odd it was that a warehouse was located so close to a residential district. He smiled and said, "This warehouse was here first . . . long before those out-of-state people descended on this town with their complicated zoning laws."

In passing, I commented on the murder up the road and asked if he had heard anything suspicious last night. He shook his head and said that he closed at five every day. He then gave me the directions I asked for.

It was time for me to go to jail.

CHAPTER EIGHT

The interrogation room in the jail at the Parrish City Hall doubled as a visitors' area. Upon entering the room, I had checked the walls, table, and seats—half in jest—for listening devices. There weren't any two-way mirrors in the room, just a framed photograph of a granite-eyed cop named Sergeant Jesse Smith, who had a handlebar mustache and wore a British-style bobby's hat. One of the pioneer cops in Parrish, Smith would probably have sneered at today's snarled court system and the concern for the rights of the accused. And he would certainly have gotten a kick out of Cate's lawyer. Probably almost as much as I did.

I sat at the end of the scarred table, scratching notes on a pad as Cate told me her story in between interruptions from her attorney, Charles "Buzz" Kerns. As she spoke, I studied her face, searching for the energetic, fresh-faced Cate of six years ago. It wasn't that the intervening years had been unkind to her. Her skin still had the smooth sheen of a woman ten years younger, and the blouse tucked neatly into her faded jeans showed off a waist even slimmer than during her days of pulling rabbits out of my hats. Perhaps what made Cate seem a stranger was the way her disheveled hair kept falling into her eyes. And how she waited a maddeningly long time before brushing it back. Perhaps it was the exhaustion in her eyes—revealed only partly by lack of makeup. The sparkle and determination of the old Cate were missing.

She had contacted Kerns because he was the only attorney she knew. He was handling her divorce. After attempting to tear my hand off while shaking it, Kerns has slipped me a plastic advertising card left over from his unsuccessful bid for a district attorney post a few years back. The flip side of the card contained a "perpetual calender"—a table for determining the day of the week for any date up to the year 2025. A cheery gift for clients facing possible prison stretches.

The freckle-faced, redheaded Kerns had a weakness for knit ties with square bottoms and coats with patched elbows. He was treating Cate's newest legal difficulty as a minor irritation. When Kerns remarked, "When your husband's attorney hears about this murder rap it's going to really gum up the divorce negotiations," Cate and I began to freeze him out of our conversation. He eventually stopped taking notes and began to fill the pages of his legal pad with doodles.

Cate sat with her chair pushed away from the table, her face rigid. Her hands gripped the arms of the chair as though she were in an astronaut's seat, preparing for a liftoff. I didn't blame her. The legal course that Buzz Kerns had advised her to take was almost as risky as a trip into space.

Cate asked, "Harry, are you sure you want me to tell the story again?"

I told her to relax and said, Yes, it was necessary to retell it. "One extra detail could break everything wide open."

"Ridiculous," Kern said. "Our time would be better spent contacting the D.A.'s office and finding out what kinds of deals they're amenable to."

It was the fifth time Kerns had used the word *amenable*. I said, "Counselor, the one thing Mrs. Fleming is *not* amenable to is spending one more day in jail than she deserves."

"Hey, we're not talking about a mere prison sentence," he said. "We're talking about life itself. Need I remind you that the state has a chair over in Rockview Prison that isn't exactly built for comfort?"

"But Cate is innocent, Mr. Kerns . . . *Buzz*. The sooner you do your job and start proving that fact, the better off she'll be."

"Your naiveté is charming, Colderwood. I used to feel that way, oh, I'd say my first year of law school. Then I wised up. Look, I know who you are. I read the papers. And I've even heard Cate speak fondly of you . . . although at the moment I can't imagine why."

I glanced at Cate, looking for a smile, but her lips were pressed together in a firm pink line. Kerns started doodling so vigorously that his pen made scraping noises. He said, "Colderwood, you've had some lucky breaks in solving a handful of crimes, but that hardly qualifies you for the rigors of a real investigation. Cate shouldn't listen to you any more than she should hire a TV doctor to perform an appendectomy.''

Cate closed her eyes, taking a long while before she reopened them. She spoke as though her jaw weighed several pounds. ''Would you both please—?''

Kerns raised his finger, about to implore her again to bargain with the D.A. I reached over and slapped my palm in the middle of Kerns's legal pad. Instead of the expected thud, there was a sickening splat. I lifted my hand to reveal a bloody handprint in the middle of the yellow page . . . even though my palm was perfectly clean. In the center of the palm print was an Ace of Spades, pointing at Kerns. He snarled as though I had just told him a revolting joke, but at least he stopped talking.

Cate said, ''I'd appreciate it if you two would stop bickering and just go about your business. Buzz, why don't you go out and talk to the arresting officers and anyone from the D.A.'s that wants to listen? It's not going to hurt to find out if they have a deal in mind. In the meantime, Harry, I'll run through my story again. You might be right, maybe I did leave something out.''

Kerns tore the ruined page from his tablet and threw it into the waste can. For all the good he was doing Cate, he might as well have tossed in his whole briefcase and jumped in after it. He dropped his legal pad into his case, slammed it shut, and locked the latches. Wishing us a good day, he marched haughtily out of the room.

Cate, her face a ghastly white, gazed for several seconds at the old photo of the cop before beginning her story again. She spoke quickly this time, as though a rapid-fire release of words would somehow ease her inner pain.

''It all started the night before last, at about 11:30. I was in my dressing room backstage at the Mount Pacifica Resort. The rest of the girls had gone, and I was alone. I was reviewing a screenplay that my agent had sent me, when I heard a knock at the door. I opened it and a man wearing a ski mask lunged in. It happened so fast . . . he never said a word. I tried to fight him off, but he was too quick. He spun me around and forced a cloth over my nose that smelled like ether. The last thing I remember was hoping that he wouldn't take the movie script I was reading. It was such a violent piece of trash, I was afraid it would give him ideas. Things went black for what seemed like only a second, and the next thing I knew, I was on my back in a small room. It was as though someone had flicked a light switch off and on. I thought we were in a motel room. The kidnapper dialed your number and shoved a typed piece of paper in front of me. At first, I thought it was from the movie script, but then I saw it was even worse—a message to you. He forced me to read it, holding a flashlight on the page. Then he put me out again. This time I woke up in a dark and clammy room.''

As I listened to her story, I mentally ticked off each detail, searching for some discrepancy from her last retelling. I struggled to keep my mind from straying as I stared at the delicate lines of her face. It was hard not to think of our years together— years when love and work had become entwined in a delicious confusion that made each day new and exciting.

In recent years there were times when I had yearned to work with her again, even if there was no longer any affection between us. Now my wish was coming true. Only this wasn't the kind of work I had in mind.

CHAPTER NINE

Cate touched a tissue to her eyes and then massaged her upper arm, wincing.

"Bruise?"

"No, it's just sore. Probably from when I struggled with the kidnapper."

I nodded and asked her to continue. With my pen clenched in my teeth, I leaned forward and rested my chin on my hands. Through several recountings, her story hadn't gotten any easier to tell. Nor—from the viewpoint of the police—any easier to believe.

Cate said that upon awakening the second time, she found herself lying on an old mattress in a cool, dark room that smelled of soap powder and furniture polish. According to her watch she had been there for nine hours. She was handcuffed to a pipe that led to a water meter. A gag kept her from calling out. She listened for evidence of movement around her, but all she could hear was the occasional sound of cars passing on a nearby road. After a lengthy ordeal of twisting and turning, she found that she could stand up by sliding the handcuffs to the uppermost part of the pipe. She hit a wall switch with her elbow, turning on an overhead cluster of three unshaded, low-watt bulbs. The cramped room had bare cinder-block walls and a low, raftered ceiling from which hung a mass of drooping cobwebs. Heaped on wooden skids around the mattress were cardboard boxes bearing the names of household appliances. There were a few sandwiches placed on a paper plate within reach. She told herself she wouldn't eat them, but it wasn't long before she was too hungry to worry about what was in them. After that, she got drowsy and slept for several hours.

Cate cursed herself for never allowing me to teach her anything about escapology during the time we worked together. She had always said that just *thinking* about being bound in ropes and chains made her panicky.

She spent the next several hours trying to stay calm. She wrestled open whatever cardboard boxes she could reach, hoping to find a weapon or a tool to extricate herself. All she found was a food blender, a steam iron, and a toaster. When her imprisonment exceeded twenty-four hours, she began to worry that no one was ever going to find her.

"At about fifteen past ten I thought I heard someone bumping around upstairs."

"Just one person?"

"At first. I heard a TV playing what sounded like one of those nighttime soap operas. Several minutes later, another set of footsteps walked into the upstairs room."

"A man or woman's?" I said.

"I couldn't tell. Soon after that an argument erupted. It was hard to distinguish their voices from the voices on TV."

"You couldn't hear their words?"

"No. They were muffled. All cheese and crackers."

"Cheese and crackers?"

"Yeah. For background conversation in movies, directors sometimes tell extras to murmur 'cheese and crackers' over and over. That's what the talking upstairs sounded like. It lasted for about five minutes."

I tried to write that down, but my pen sputtered and stopped. I shook it, wet the tip with my tongue, and scratched it across the page. It still wouldn't write.

"Why not use some of your famous magic on the pen, Harry?" Cate's sarcasm sent a chill down my back. "Isn't that what it always comes to when the going gets rugged? You just pull out your trusty magic wand and make everything right again."

I pressed the pen to the tabletop and dragged it along, leaving a groove that was hardly noticeable among the carved graffiti. It still wouldn't write.

"I've really thrown you a curveball this time, Harry. So what's your game plan? Are you going to spring me from this joint right away or are you going to cook up a grandstand play?"

I held the point of the pen under the flame of my cigarette lighter. When it was on the verge of melting, I withdrew the heat. Then I fired up a cigarette, knowing it would make Cate grimace, perhaps sparking another of her health lectures. I tried the pen again. Still dead.

"Hey," I said, "I could bust you out of here right now if that's what you really want. On the way in I cased the setup. In the rear of the building is a staff-only elevator with a single-key lock that's a piece of cake. And I noticed that the lock on the holding pen is ancient . . . hasn't been changed since the 1920's. Your cell lock is probably the same vintage. With enough distraction—perhaps a bomb threat—it would be a snap to slip you past the guard and down the back way. We could make Mexico in a few days. Now, as for our alternatives"—she arched her eyebrows doubtfully—"we could try to clear your name by figuring out who set you up. But that'll take time—and finesse. And you can bet that your lawyer, Buzz, will be underfoot every step of the way."

"But Buzz is—"

"A jerk. A small-time divorce lawyer and ambulance chaser. The only thing he sees in you is a ticket into the limelight of criminal work. He's so convinced that you're guilty, he won't even try to dig up evidence to the contrary. Right now Buzz is probably out in the squad room playing footsie with the cops."

"You think Buzz would sell me out? He's really gone to bat for me during the divorce proceedings."

"I guarantee he'd sell you out. Only he wouldn't call it that. He'd use a phrase like 'facing reality.' Which, come to think of it, is the opposite of what *I* do for a living, isn't it?"

Cate shook her head. "You're wrong. Buzz has been good to me."

"Buzz is good at cutting quick and fancy deals. But for that you'd be better off hiring your theatrical agent as your lawyer. I'm sure Buzz is very charming, and spends many Saturday nights in the company of grateful divorcees. But if you need proof of what he's really like . . ." I pulled from my pocket a felt-tipped pen and a napkin from the Anchor Coffee Shop. I wrote on the napkin with bold strokes, and passed it to Cate. She tried to hide her smile, but finally let it radiate across her face. I had forgotten how much I missed that smile. It made the room seem suddenly much warmer.

"Give me your pen," she said. I handed her the felt-tipped one, but she said, "No. The ballpoint. The one that quit writing." She pretended to pinch magic dust out of the air and sprinkle it on the pen. In a sendup of my performing style, she waved her hand a foot away from the pen, as though transmitting invisible waves. Taking a clean sheet of paper from my notepad, she glided the pen along the bottom. It left an easy blue line, rich and constant with no skips.

"Voilà," she said. "Now *that's* magic."

"Why, uh, not really, Cate. You see, there's a logical explanation." I hastily took back the pen, clicked it, and shoved it into my pocket. "It probably started writing again because it absorbed my body heat when I was holding it. Yeah, that's it—body heat. Plus, we can't discount the cumulative effect of all my moving around, which—"

"Spare me the logic, please." Cate's smile had faded, and the lines at the corners of her eyes looked deeper and harder. I felt the glow of nostalgia ebbing away. "Harry, for once can't you forget your rules of rational thinking? Can't you just admit that I performed a tiny miracle?"

I gave her a shrug and swung open the door to the interrogation room. Looking out into the squad room, we could see Buzz Kerns sitting on a swivel desk chair in front of a semicircle of plainclothes men. He hadn't wasted any time. Kerns was playing liar's poker with them, and—judging from the pile of dollar bills on the desk behind the cops—they were taking him to the cleaners. Kerns looked up and winked at me, letting me know that he was winning their confidence by letting them win his money. When Kerns looked down for a moment, the cop sitting across from him winked at me—obviously, he and his buddies were onto Kerns's game and were making the most of the opportunity.

Cate moved her chair to the side so that she didn't have to look at Kerns. She glanced up at the picture of Sergeant Jesse Smith, whose expression seemed even sterner. We heard Kerns groan and say, "Come on, guys. Give me a break."

In a small voice, Cate said, "I guess I'd better finish my story."

I closed the door. "You told me that the talking upstairs stopped at what time?"

"About ten-thirty. That's when I heard the shot."

"The TV was off by then?"

She thought for a few seconds. "Yes, I think it was. After the shot, there was a long silence. No more moving around or talking. Then after more footsteps, the TV voices returned. Whoever did the shooting must have switched it back on. A few minutes later, the steps grew louder. They sounded like they were coming downstairs to where I was. The door suddenly flew open, and standing in the doorway was a person dressed in a black coat, carrying a gun.''

''The same one who kidnapped you?''

''I think so. He was wearing the same ski mask. Because of that, I knew he wasn't going to kill me.''

''Why?''

''Because it meant that he was still afraid I could identify him.''

''Do you remember anything about his gun?''

''I'd never seen a pistol quite like it. It was black, but it looked phony. Like a cartoon gun. But that was probably just my imagination working overtime, due to stress.''

''What did he do next?''

''He removed my handcuffs, took off my gag, and shoved me down on the mattress. I thought he was going to attack me, but he simply turned and walked out, locking the door behind him. Not long after, the cops showed up and charged me with the murder of Lisa South. Only then did I learn I had been held prisoner in the basement of her house. They found her body in the middle of her living room rug, a bullet in the back of her head. When they searched her place, the police were amazed at the weapons and security devices hidden everywhere. Apparently they didn't do her a bit of good. They didn't find the murder weapon.''

''Did the cops contact your husband?''

''Yes, they called Phil. He has an ironclad alibi. Even though the affair between Lisa and him was long over, the police thought it was still enough motive for me to commit murder. I have never even met the woman before!''

Coffee cup in hand, Kerns walked back into the room. He slid his wallet back into his jacket pocket as he sat on the tabletop between Cate and me. He said, ''You two still determined to cling to that kidnap story?''

''Yep,'' Cate said. ''Call us old-fashioned. We're sticking to the truth.''

Eyes full of skepticism, he said, ''It wouldn't hurt if you had something else old-fashioned on your side . . . like one shred of evidence to back up your cockamamie story.''

I pushed the napkin from the coffee shop toward him. "How's this for starters? I found it this morning on the front seat of my van.''

Crimson flooded Kerns's face as he read the words I had scrawled on the napkin: *Mr. Colderwood, don't talk to the cops or I guarantee that you and the woman will die. But feel free to talk to Cate Fleming's lawyer. He doesn't worry me at all. I need a good laugh.*

Kerns smoothed out the napkin and tucked it inside his coat. I asked, "What are you going to do with it?"

"What do you suggest?" he asked in a condescending tone.

"You might consult a handwriting analyst and have him work up a psychological profile on the kidnapper."

"Will do," he said with an attempt at sincerity. He bade Cate a theatrical farewell, putting his hand on her shoulder and promising to get to work on her bail proceedings. She slid out from under his touch.

After he left, Cate said, "I don't get it. You always said that handwriting analysis is bunk."

"Oh, I still think it is. Right up there with biorhythms and trance-channelers who claim that dead people have entered their bodies. I just wanted to give Kerns something to gnaw on . . . while you and I do some real work."

I folded over another page of my notepad. "Think you could run through your story again? Last time, I promise."

I would have liked it better if she had raised a fuss, but she just sighed and started her tale from the top, reciting the words that had become rote from being repeated so many times in this stale little room.

As I took notes with the ballpoint pen that Cate had resurrected, I decided that my first step would be to attack the case from the other end—from *my* involvement in it.

I was going to track down some old poker buddies.

CHAPTER TEN

The man beside me wore a golfer's hat pulled low over what I imagined to be a bald head. Hanging from his neck was a camera with a lens attachment so big that it looked like a nasty weapon. He leaned an elbow on the photo-shop counter and thumbed lovingly through his stack of pictures. Then he saw me and came over, proudly displaying his work. Most of his snapshots were girls on the beach in Atlantic City—something like a *Playboy* pictorial. Interspersed were several shots of a scowling woman wearing huge sunglasses and a bikini that just might have fit five years ago. She seemed a bit peeved by her husband's straying shutter finger.

As I dodged the man's lascivious nudging, the clerk returned with my packet of pictures. I peeled open the flap and fanned through the photos. Feeling someone's breath on my shoulder, I turned to see the man in shorts standing on tiptoe behind me. It appeared that since he had subjected me to his travelogue, he felt entitled to review the highlights of *my* vacation.

I stuffed the pictures back in the envelope and began to head for the door when I changed my mind. I went back and handed the man my envelope, figuring that I had nothing to lose. If he was a native of Parrish, there was a chance he might know some of my fellow poker players. As he reviewed my pictures, he groaned softly and shook his head. There were no bathing beauties, sandy beaches, redwood trees, or amusement park rides, just a lot of unfocused, poorly framed shots of people playing cards.

He smiled condescendlingly and patted my shoulder. "Don't feel bad, buddy. I used to take crappy pictures, too. Just keep at it. Pretty soon you'll learn to hold your camera higher and

steadier." He took another mournful look at the pictures. "It's a wonder you got any passable shots. What kind of film did you use?"

"Beats me. I used the roll that came with the camera."

"Ah, now, *that* was your first mistake. What kind of camera?"

"Damned if I know. There's no brand name on it. The camera looks exactly like a tie pin. That way you can take pictures without people knowing it."

The man's smile slowly evaporated. He dropped his hand from my shoulder and wiped it on the side of his shorts. Looking as though he had just remembered a pressing appointment, he turned on his heel and headed for the door muttering something under his breath about crazy strangers. I called after him. "Did you happen to recognize anybody in the pictures?" He shook his head and walked out onto the sidewalk, his baggy shorts flapping in the breeze and his knobby knees coming very close to knocking.

Back at the jail again, I showed Cate the pictures. As she studied each one, the effort of concentration cut deep lines into her forehead. "No, I don't know any of these people."

"None of them looks even vaguely familiar?"

She nibbled her lower lip. "No, but who's to say that I didn't briefly glimpse one of them before? Maybe one of them was even on the same bus with me when I arrived in town a few weeks ago. Who knows? Nobody has a memory that keen."

Which gave me an idea.

He billed himself as *Mr. Memory, the Man with the Steel-Trap Mind.* One sniff told me that he hadn't forgotten to have a drink this morning—one of the many benefits of a photographic memory. He was wearing a frayed tuxedo—purchased from the closeout rack of a rental shop—and a thousand-dollar snow-white toupee with more swirls than a deluxe cone of soft ice cream. A weak chin and thin lips conveyed the impression that he was always worrying over some momentous decision.

As part of his act at the Mystic Isle, Mr. Memory greeted all the guests while they stood in line to be seated. Later, onstage, he gave a rapid-fire recitation of all their names, matching them with the faces in the audience. He didn't rely on

mnemonic tricks; he had a rare photographic memory. His mind was the equivalent of an endless videotape that permanently stored all he saw and heard . . . whether he liked it or not. Mr. Memory considered his ability a curse. Unlike most people, painful experiences didn't fade away to the dark recesses of his mind. Every unpleasant event in his life was etched into his brain and lay dormant, awaiting a cue to be relived in full, awful detail. Mr. Memory often resorted to alcohol to dull bitter memories of the past.

If Mr. Memory had ever seen any of the people in my pictures—even for just an instant—he would recall exactly when and where. However, after poring over my envelope of photos, his face remained blank. He shook his head. "Sorry, wish I could help. The fact is, I don't meet many people outside of the club. In general, I try not to clutter my mind. I hardly watch TV, and God forbid if I were to start reading newspapers again. You see, depression is an occupational hazard for me. It's the images of people in pain that haunt me the most. Just give me a dark barroom with empty stools on either side and a full glass in front of me . . . and every once in a while I feel almost happy. The trick is to insulate myself as much as possible from negativity."

"Believe me," I said, fanning the pictures, "one of these people is responsible for a lot of negativity. A hell of a lot."

Showing the pictures to Mr. Memory had been a hunch that didn't pay off. What was my next step? Would I take to the streets, handing out copies of the photos, like pictures of runaways?

I was lying across my hotel room bed, resting up for tonight's show. As I mulled over my options, the phone rang. It was Mr. Memory. "Harry. I was wrong. I mean, I was right."

"Make up your mind, Mr. M. Which is it?"

"Oh no, you've got it ass-backwards. I *never* make up my mind. It's all quite the opposite." He lost himself in a long laugh that ended in a hiccup. "When you showed me the pictures, you asked me to concentrate on the people's faces."

"Do you recognize one of them now?"

"No, I still haven't the foggiest who they are. But a few minutes ago it hit me. It's the *background* in your pictures that I've seen before—that game room where you played poker. You

see, I saw that game room for the first time when I was in a bar-room . . .''

I lit a cigarette, bracing myself for his drink-induced ram-bling. As he talked I heard a record playing in the background. It sounded like Bob Hope's theme. I swear.

CHAPTER ELEVEN

"It was three days ago, exactly," Mr. Memory said. "The beer clock above the bar said 5:47 P.M."

"You're sure you were in a bar when you saw the game room?" I was wondering how much of his recollection he'd gotten from the bottom of a bottle.

"Positive. The TV above the bar was playing, and there on the screen, true as life, was the game room in your photos."

"What show was playing?"

"I didn't see the title, but the program was one of those dreadful little films set to popular songs."

"Music videos?" I said.

"Right, right. Music videos. Your game room was a setting for one of those videos. Like I said, it took me a long time to make the connection because your pictures were blurry and because I had concentrated too damn hard on the people's faces. I guess my own vision, while in the barroom, was also a bit blurred."

"Do you remember what music group recorded the video?"

"Sorry, I can't remember something I didn't see. I only glanced up at the TV screen for a few seconds before someone switched channels. That music was terrible—just thinking about it hurts my ears. Harry, if it helps, I remember what channel it was on."

He told me the channel. I thanked him and asked again if he was sure it was the same game room as in my pictures.

"Hey, 'memory' is my middle name."

"No, it's your last name," I said, hanging up and wondering how he could forget such a thing.

* * *

54

The TV station was based in Allentown. The receptionist who answered the phone consulted her listings and told me that the show Mr. Memory had seen was called *Smash Music*. Unable to tell me what videos aired during the show, she gave me the phone number of the program's production company, Polar Vision.

A secretary at Polar Vision told me that the name of the video was "Lucky Dead Men" and it was recorded by a group called Aces High. She referred me to the record company that had released the video. Soon I was speaking to a man from New York City named Bill Barthman, the director of the video. Barthman sounded groggy and I apologized for waking him. Bewildered, he said that he hadn't been asleep. I wondered how a director so lethargic could ever bring a video in under budget, on deadline.

Pretending that I was a student trying to break into the business, I started asking him questions about shooting and editing techniques. He seemed flattered that I took his work so seriously. After a few minutes, I slipped in a question about "Lucky Dead Men."

While waiting for him to answer, I heard the sound of liquid being poured into a glass, followed by plinking ice cubes. "Oh *that* one," he said, some of the weariness gone from his voice. "You must be kidding. Someone is actually playing that piece of crap? Jeez, we put the wraps on it only a week and a half ago. A real rush job. We cranked it out in one three-hour session on an impossibly low budget, with practically no editing. I was tempted to remove my name from the credits."

"Where did you shoot 'Lucky Dead Men?' "

"In the Village, at the Cry By Night Studios, which is actually a huge loft partitioned off into small sound stages. Not many companies shoot videos there. It's usually rented out to a syndicate of high rollers who churn out adult films at assembly-line pace. I thought my colleagues in videos and TV commercials worked fast, but these porn dudes wrote the book on quick and cheap."

"But surely you didn't shoot it in a studio. That game room in the video was real, wasn't it?"

"That's an interesting point," Barthman said. "Since we were on a tight budget, you're probably wondering why our set was so richly detailed."

"Exactly."

"You can blame that extravagance on a guy named Milan Posar, the manager of Aces High. A couple days before shooting—for no apparent reason—Posar insisted on taking control of the project. He's never done that before. All he usually cares about is grinding his groups down, always hounding them to bring in more cash—either by touring or by cutting more records. He has a reputation for being cheap, always trying to get everything in one take. Videos usually don't generate enough money to interest him, but for this one, Posar blew nearly every cent in the budget on that game room set. There was so little money left for studio time that we had only a half day to shoot it. The result was so shoddy; I told Posar it would never get on the air. And you know what? He said he didn't care. If you ask me, I think the guy's burned out from too many years in the business."

"What kind of groups does Posar manage?"

"The kind that come from nowhere and hit with top-forty records that get hourly airplay on every major radio station in the country for five weeks . . . and then drop out of sight, usually never heard from again. Occasionally one of his groups achieves success, but it's always *after* they leave Posar. Musicians who survive him chalk it up as an experience in learning how low and dirty this business can get. His groups usually end up as opening acts for sleazy rock revival shows. He has the uncanny knack for knowing just when to jettison an act—after wringing the last possible dollar out of them."

"Do you know how I can get hold of him?"

"You really do want to learn this business from the ground up, don't you? You can try, but he'll probably brush you off. The last thing he'll want to do is hold a career day for a wet-behind-the-ears college kid. Maybe you can wangle his phone number from his record company. Even so, you probably won't reach him. He doesn't live in New York all the time. While I was shooting the video, all he talked about was getting back to some place called Paris."

"Parrish?"

"Yeah. Could be. I think he has a summer home there."

I thanked him for his information and hung up, thinking that this was interesting information indeed.

Because the station in Allentown had told me that airing of *Smash Music* was scheduled for today, I called Ed McClenahan, a stagehand at the Mystic Isle, and asked him to record the show on the club's video cassette recorder.

A few hours later I was at the Isle, watching Posar's video, "Lucky Dead Men," over and over again. After the first viewing, I grew tired of the repetitive lyrics and endless guitar solos, so I turned the volume down. The story line centered on a surrealistic poker game played by classic horror-movie monsters: Frankenstein, Dracula, the Mummy, and the Wolf Man. Closeups revealed that the cards in their hands contained animated images of ordinary people trying desperately to escape from their two-dimensional prisons.

Mr. Memory's powers of recall had not failed him. The card game was being played in what seemed to be the same game room where I had played poker. The doors were in the right place. The walls were the right color. I saw the same dart board and compact disc system. Even a glimpse of the powder room could be seen through the open door at the end of the room. But certain elements were distorted. For example, the round poker table was twice as big as the one I had played at. The darts stuck in the dart board were actually daggers. And the room was lit by candles that cast unearthly shadows about the room. These exaggerations provided another explanation why the literal-minded Mr. Memory had not immediately made the connection between the video and my pictures.

I leafed through the local phone book chained to the pay phone in the basement of the club. The only Posar in the Parrish directory had the initials M.P. The address was a rural route. Rather than try to locate his house, I took a chance and dialed the number.

An answering machine kicked in after one ring and informed me that I had reached the residence of Milan Posar and that he couldn't come to the phone. Twice the voice stumbled over words and in the middle of the message, there was a rude coughing. Apparently Posar believed in recording only one take even when it came to his answering machine. At the sound of the beep, I said, "My name is Harry. I played poker with you the other night. I'd like to have a little chat with you. About Lisa South."

Suddenly Posar's voice came on the line, live. "Sorry, I couldn't make it to the machine in time to turn it off. You say your name's Harry?"

When I told him yes, he gave me detailed directions on how to find his house. He sounded relieved.

CHAPTER TWELVE

Following Posar's directions, I turned off the highway when I spotted a sign with a big hunting arrow pointing the way to the now defunct Parrish Sportsman's Club. The narrow dirt road went through a tunnel that burrowed through an embankment over which railroad tracks ran.

Emerging from the tunnel, I found myself in a bleaker world than that of the elegant summer homes that dotted the main highway. The houses on this side were closely grouped cottages, originally intended to provide a summer escape from the din and dirt of the city. But they were now year-round homes for many of the victims of Parrish's economic woes.

I took a jouncing ride over a bridge made of railroad ties that spanned a dried-up creek. Posar's cottage lay at the end of the road, where a turnaround loop cut through the edge of a ragged orchard. Posar's mailbox bore no name. His lawn, not mowed in weeks, rippled like wheat.

Parked at the entrance to his driveway was a ten-year-old Buick, freckled with rust. The edges of the windshield were coated with grime and splattered insects. Behind the wheel sat a man wearing a mournful expression and a straw hat shoved back. He looked up from his newspaper, giving me a critical stare as he ran me by some mental checklist, giving me a barely passing okay. He was obviously locally hired muscle, the kind who advertised in the Yellow Pages under the guise of a private detective. He didn't return my friendly nod.

Posar's cottage, with its loose shingles and torn shades, looked more like a hideout than a hideaway. It was shedding its paint like a bad sunburn. The front porch was screened in on all sides but because the screens were filthy, I didn't press my face close enough to see inside. I knocked, and a voice bellowed for me to walk in. Posar must have had a lot of confidence in his body-guard—he didn't even ask who I was.

The cottage consisted of only three rooms—kitchen, living room, and bedroom. Posar had converted the living room into an office. Clutter from his business was heaped on every available surface: glossy eight-by-tens of baby-faced rockers with evil glares, cassette tapes with scribbled labels, and stacks of record albums with *Promotional Use Only* stickers. Contracts and legal papers were scattered everywhere. Unopened mail lay on the floor, filling one corner of the room like drifted snow.

Wearing loose-fitting surfer's shorts and leather sandals with black socks, Milan Posar was sprawled on a reclining chair, the footrest cranked straight out. As I had suspected, Milan Posar was the poker player who called himself Miles. Speaking into the phone nestled against his shoulder, he scraped the bottom of a yogurt cup. In between spoonfuls, he nodded and said, "Yeah" and "Uh-uh."

He gestured for me to have a seat on the couch and smiled sheepishly when he realized there wasn't room—his couch was currently serving as an open-air file cabinet. I pushed aside a stack of folders and sat down. On the wall behind me I saw a framed news clipping of a slimmer Milan Posar presiding over the signing of a major recording deal with a bearded young man in a rugby shirt. I remembered the kid's name from a monster-hit song about five years ago, but I couldn't remember hearing anything from him since. Similar pictures lined the wall. The only significant differences between the photos were the number of sharp teeth exposed by Posar's lupine grin.

His eyes fierce but also oddly playful, Posar was nearly shout-ing into his phone. "You guys have a good thing going with your first album. Why do you want to blow it? You better stick to your formula or you'll confuse your fans. Huh? What do you mean, *passé?* Believe me, car crash songs *are* making a comeback." He rolled his eyes at me and swallowed another spoonful of yogurt. "Of course I know who Pete Best was. Oh, no, what are you trying to tell me?" Snickering, he clamped his hand to the mouthpiece and said to me, "These clowns think they're the next Beatles. They want me to fire their drummer because they think he's holding them back from superstardom. They can only wish!" He spoke again into the phone. "Artie, let's make a deal. If you want me to, I'll fire Bruce. But only under two conditions: first, instead of replacing him, I want you to use computerized percussion; second, I want Bruce's cut of all future money. Huh? What do you mean highway robbery? Just consider it payment due me for doing your dirty work."

It became obvious that Artie was now having second thoughts about firing the drummer. When he hung up, Posar was shaking his head. He clasped his hands behind his head and laughed. "Wow, that Artie was sure bent out of shape."

Posar chuckled to himself for a few moments, then he stared at me. He pulled the lever, and with a sharp twang of springs the chair snapped to an upright position like a soldier bolting to attention. "I take it you're in the same business?"

"Not exactly. But you remind me of a former manager of mine. After I did eight shows on the Fourth of July at a theme park, he tried to stiff me for my fee. The fireworks at the park that night were nothing compared to the ones we shot off. The judge later ordered me to never darken his doorway again."

Posar searched through the mire of papers, cassette tapes, and trade magazines on the coffee table until he found a pair of eyeglasses. As recognition spread across his face, I quickly told him who I was and what I did for a living. He gave his clenched fist a little shake as everything fell into place.

"Sure, I remember you now," he said. "You had a TV special about five or six years ago, right?"

"Almost," I said. "There was a hell of a flap when I discovered that the network programming chief was relying on a fortune-teller for advice on scheduling shows."

Posar's smile turned oily. "Boy-oh-boy, you had those slimy bastards right where you wanted them. What'd you do?" He stabbed the air with an invisible knife and pretended to twist the handle. "How bad did you shake them down?"

"Uh, I didn't get a dime, actually. All I did was call a press conference and blow the whistle on them."

Posar's eyes grew round, as though he had watched a baseball umpire make an atrociously bad call. "You *what?* You actually told the tr—" Somehow I knew that the word *truth* would make him choke. He cleared his throat and said, "Talk about a real deal-blower, man."

"That's exactly right. I blew not only that deal, but, it seems, my whole future—sky high. They canceled my special and sealed the master tape of the show in a can. It's now molding away in some network vault.''

''So how the hell did you wind up playing two-bit dumps like the Mystic Isle? They blacklisted you, right?''

''Yeah. The word spread that I was unreliable, someone who wouldn't play ball. The talk shows stopped booking me for guest shots. Without TV, it's easy to develop the 'has-been' label.''

Posar glanced around at his photo shrine of one-hit wonders and said, ''Hey, you don't have to tell me how fast the public forgets. I once handled a guy who went from standing in a New Orleans unemployment line to a Number-Nineteen-With-a-Bullet song on *Billboard* and then back to that same line again, all before his unemployment claim expired. Why, I once took a couple of sisters who worked in a jacket factory in Kansas City and . . .''

As he reminisced about his former clients, I at first thought he was being wistful about the fickle public; but as he continued, I realized that his only regret was how long it took him to develop a sense of when to dump a client.

After a few moments he began to notice that I was nodding merely to be polite. Even though we were both in show business, we were on opposite sides of the fence. He soon lapsed into a sullen silence. After several seconds, he raised an accusing finger at me. ''Of course! Your magic won that damn poker game for you!'' His face showed his confusion as he wondered how I could have crippled my TV career for principles he only vaguely understood, while I still used my magic to bilk strangers in a card game.

''Milan, I was there against my will last night. I was trying to save the life of a friend.'' I told him about my mission to raise ransom money and how it ended with Cate's being charged with murder. After explaining how I tracked him down, I said, ''Now that I've told you what I know, I'd appreciate it if you'd do the same. How about if we start with the game room itself. Do you have any idea where it's located? Or who organized the game?''

He rubbed his fingertip along his heavy browbone. ''Last night was the fourth time we played together. The same limo that picked up Nicole, John, and you was also the one that drove me to the game earlier. During all those games, I never got a chance to look around the house. The doors were always locked, except for those leading from the garage to the game room. Prior to our first game, I had never laid eyes on any of the other players. It all started with an invitation in the mail. I—'' Anticipating my next question, he opened an end table drawer. Papers and envelopes sprang out over the edges. Like a mail clerk in an insane asylum, he sorted through the layers of envelopes, tossing in the air the ones he didn't want. He stopped when he came to a three-by-five-inch matted card with ragged edges. He handed it to me, and when I opened it, I was staring at a note produced on a computer printer, like the ransom note for Cate:

Dear Mr. Posar:

We cordially invite you to compete in a weekly poker game with three other players. We're sure you'll find the stakes attractive. There are no betting limits and no house cut. If you are interested, bring $15,000 to the corner of Webster and Forbes at 8:30 P.M., July 12.

Our rules are simple: you must respect the anonymity of the group and use first names only. Also, you must keep your participation a secret. Any attempt to find the location of the playing site or the organizer of the game will result in its cancellation. Hope to see you there. Good luck.

I returned the card to him. Like the rest of his mail, he gave it a toss, not caring where it landed. I said, ''So you took an envelope full of money to a strange street corner at night? With no precautions?''

He shook his head. ''You think I'm nuts? I took precautions. Look around. You think I have vast sums of cash tucked away, just waiting to be invested? Uh-uh. I don't work that way. For me, saving money is like trying to fill up a sink with the stopper pulled out. I'd walk away from the music business tomorrow if I could. But you tell me how else I could live like this.'' He gestured proudly around the room, assuming that I envied his life-style. ''Oh, I smelled fish on this invitation, all right. A whole school of fish. But I also smelled cash . . . *if* I played it right. This operation had the feel of an amateur, someone who loved the idea of intrigue but didn't have the nerve to face real danger. I decided to take a chance. So I called in a few markers and also told some white lies to a few friends who are still naive enough to trust me. It didn't take long to raise the capital. As for my precaution . . ."

Posar parted the curtain of the window behind him to give me a view of the old Buick parked along the road. When I looked quizzically at Posar, he turned to see that the man behind the wheel was gone. He put his face to the screen and bellowed, "Johnson! Johnson! What the hell am I paying you for?" The man with the straw hat shot to a sitting position, fighting his way through a blanket of newspaper.

Posar let the curtain drop back. "Johnson runs a detective agency. He's a good man, but he needs sleep right now. He just came off a thirty-six-hour stakeout for a divorce case. After you called me today, I phoned and asked him to keep an eye on things around here. I've used him off and on for a couple years. In my profession you never know when a skeleton's going to come boogying out of the closet." He smiled widely and scratched his beard. "Not for a minute did I consider going to that first poker game without some kind of protection."

"So Johnson tailed you to the first game?"

"Well, he *tried* to tail me. A limousine—the same one that took me to last night's game—picked me up at the corner of Webster and Forbes. After cruising a few blocks, the chauffeur must have spotted Johnson's Buick several cars back. He took evasive measures that had me flying from side to side. A few minutes later, our speed dropped back down. When I checked with Johnson the next day, he said that limo driver was a real pro. No one had ever shaken him so quickly."

I wondered if Johnson was simply unused to detective work requiring more subtlety than the flash of a handgun or a crack to the jaw.

"Was that first poker game played in the same game room as last night?" I asked.

"Yeah. Same people, too. From the start, it was apparent that the dude named John had received more detailed instructions than the rest of us. He immediately assumed the job of banker, doling out the poker chips and cards. Two hands into that first game, I realized I was onto something good—*too* good to be true. I knew I could beat those other players any night of the week . . . even blindfolded. It was a bonanza. The next day I called Johnson and told him I wouldn't need him anymore. I didn't want to blow what might amount to a personal gold mine."

Posar was hunched forward in his chair, his elbows on his knees and his hands clasped together. His hushed tone reminded me of a camp-fire storyteller.

I said, "With all that easy money, why make the video? Why take a chance of screwing up a good thing?"

"After that first poker game, I began having recurring nightmares. Deep down, I probably thought that someone was setting me up for a fall. In spite of the nightmares, I showed up religiously every week at that same street corner, an envelope of money tucked in my jacket, all ready to quadruple itself. And the dreams got worse. I thought that if I wrote the whole dream down on paper, it might loosen its grip on me. Then I got the inspiration to do more than that. When one of my groups was scheduled to shoot a quickie video, I took advantage of the opportunity. I dictated the details of my dream to the director, and worked closely with the set designer, recreating the game room as it appeared in my nightmare. Ordinarily music is strictly a business to me. I never interfere with the creativity—if you want to call it that—of my groups. But I desperately wanted to get rid of those nightmares."

"Did it work?"

Posar shook his head as if amused by his folly. "No. In fact the dreams got worse and I began to lose even more sleep."

"Now that you know that the poker game is somehow connected with Lisa South's death, your nights aren't going to get any shorter, are they?" His eyes darted away from mine and focused on a point behind and above my head. "Tell me, Milan, did you know Lisa South?"

He pinched the front of his shirt and pulled it away from his chest as though my sticky question had actually made him feel sticky. "Yeah. We knew each other. At one time we were even friends."

He was still looking into the distance. His voice became wooden and his words formal. "I met Lisa six years ago out on the Coast. At that time she was a nobody . . . just a reporter for a small newspaper that was more like a shopper's guide than a real paper. And I wasn't much different than I am now: a third-class hustler, sleeping and eating in a tiny office, sharing the fifth floor with a dentist who never used Novocain and an insurance man whose file cabinet was a size-ten shoe box. During those days I was surviving on promises and lies, keeping my phone off the hook when things got heavy. At first, my interest in Lisa was strictly limited to getting her into the bedroom. Even back then Lisa South knew exactly what she was doing—she knew instinctively which strings to pull, and how much to tease me to keep my hopes up. In addition to human-interest pieces and cooking articles, she was writing a weekly column about the entertainment industry. She soon had me supplying her with tales about celebrities that I'd heard at parties. On the strength of the stuff I gave her, her writing began to draw attention from legitimate newspapers, one of which offered her a temporary post. It turned into a permanent job and a few other papers picked up her column. By then, I'd accepted the fact that she and I were never going to share her bed. I also began to see a glimmer of hope for her career. Sure enough, the trickle of newspapers that ran her column soon became a flood. Long after she developed her own sources, I kept feeding her tips, and in return, she occasionally gave favorable reviews of the acts I handled. Our relationship settled down into an easy friendship. We felt bound together by our unique ability to mine people's talents for our own benefit.''

I asked, ''So what finally broke it up between you?''

Posar covered his mouth and coughed lightly. ''We grew apart gradually. It all started when Lisa signed a contract to do celebrity interviews for local newscasts around the country. The critics praised her uncanny ability to get reclusive personalities to open up on-camera. Her TV success garnered serious attention for her columns, and the critics were surprised to find that she was actually a good writer. Around this time her relationship with me started to become an embarrassment for her. She seemed to think that she was too good for me. When she started working on her first network special, she began ignoring my phone calls. Our relationship deteriorated rapidly. A month ago I was out in L.A. to audition a new group working the club-and-bar circuit. I was having dinner at a crowded restaurant when I noticed Lisa South sitting alone. I stopped by and said hello, but she looked straight through me, as if I was a cloud of smoke. I tried to strike up a conversation, thinking that perhaps I could score a few column inches for the new group, but as I was speaking, she excused herself to go to the ladies' room. That's when I flipped out! I started screaming and calling her names. I could almost hear the other gossip columnists clicking their ballpoint pens and taking notes. Out of nowhere two bouncers appeared. They did a discreet strong-arm number on me, showing me the door.''

"Do you remember what you yelled at her?"

"Oh, I didn't say much, I was pretty speechless with fury. I think I said, 'I'm going to strangle you. Where do you get off thinking that you're now so much better than me? Don't forget I knew you when you were nothing! My help got you here.' Et cetera, et cetera. Harmless stuff like that.''

"Did reports of your tiff appear in any of the gossip columns?''

"Nope. It didn't get even one mention. Professional courtesy, I suppose. But I'm sure the news spread throughout the grapevine. If the police interview the right people, it won't take long to find out about me.'' His face was the color of the ash on my cigarette.

"Have any idea who the other players are?" I asked.

"No, they were very secretive. But I can tell you this: that old guy, Les, and that broad, Nicole, were playing strictly for enjoyment. And as for John, he's even hungrier for money than I am—so hungry, it jinxed his playing.''

I pretended to get up to leave, but then pulled out my notepad and started scribbling. Posar took a deep breath and spoke earnestly. "Okay, Harry, I know what you're thinking . . . that somehow I sneaked away from that game, offed Lisa, and made it back without anyone missing me. Yeah, I noticed—as I'm sure you did—that someone monkeyed with that bathroom window. But any of the players could have done that. Trouble is, I'm the only one you tracked down so far. And, conveniently, I also happen to have a motive. I wish I could help you locate the others, but the only one I have a theory about is Nicole. And— mind you—it's must a theory.''

"What's that?''

"I think she's a prostitute.''

Before I could answer, he cut me off. "No, I'm not talking about any twenty-five-dollar streetwalker. I mean a high-class call girl.''

"Why do you say that?''

"I base my judgment partly on my personal experience''—his smile was devilish—"and partly on the way she talked. A couple of times she referred to her poker chips as her *stash* and then seemed to catch herself. She also seemed to take delight in calling John by name . . . as if it was a joke that only she could understand. I also take into account her appearance—at each game she came dressed entirely too sexy for the occasion. Also, when she was digging in her purse, I spotted a phone beeper. Now why the hell would she be carrying a pocket pager? Because she's a doctor? Or an undertaker? Tell you what I think. I think her work requires her to be constantly on call. Judging from the way she dresses, what business do *you* think she's in?''

I nodded at his logic, made a quick note on my pad, and put it away. As I headed for the door, he said, ''I hope you find Lisa's killer. Until then, my nightmares will probably get worse.''

As I showed myself out, Posar's phone rang and he started talking to a singing duo that had two surfing hits twenty-five years ago. They were planning to quit their jobs as hairstylists and get back into the music business. They felt that Milan Posar would be the perfect manager for them. I couldn't have agreed more.

Outside, I picked a wildflower and slipped its stem between the interlocked fingers of Johnson, the sleeping detective. I was about to steal quietly away, but changed my mind. I reached through the car window and nudged him awake.

''What do you want?'' he said in a growl. He tossed the flower out the window, making sure that I glimpsed the pistol in his shoulder holster. Well, I thought, he's used up one trick in his arsenal. I stepped back in case he tried to use the other one: a crack to the jaw.

''I need some information,'' I said. ''And I have a feeling you're just the man to ask. Tell me, Johnson, what's the best call-girl service in town?''

CHAPTER THIRTEEN

The two phone numbers that Johnson gave me were dead ends. When I called the first, the woman who answered said she was a clerk at the local Mom and Pop's all-night convenience store. The second was a dial-a-joke service specializing in sophomoric ethnic humor. A favorite, I'm sure, of Johnson's.

Sitting in my hotel room, staring at the floorboards peeking through the holes in the carpet, I mulled over my next move. All I knew about Nicole was that she liked to play poker, that she was a stunning, statuesque blonde, and that Milan Posar had her pegged as a call girl. I didn't know where to start.

So I called Room Service and ordered a bucket of ice.

The bellhop, in his early thirties, looked experienced enough to answer my questions. He eyed the playing cards, palming coins, and loud scarfs scattered across my bed. His gaze also took in the pile of ivory-tipped magic wands that lay tangled like jackstraws on my dresser. After smoothly pocketing my generous tip, he seemed to sense that I was about to make an unusual request.

When I winked and told him I was interested in finding a date—someone who really wanted to have a good time—he relaxed and flashed me a knowing smile. Sure, maybe I was more eccentric than the average hotel guest, with my flower darts stuck deeply into the wood of the bathroom door and my double wrist chopper standing ominously in the corner. But, hell, I wasn't any different than the scores of other men who had taken him aside and requested some extra-special room service.

He reassessed my appearance and my belongings, trying to estimate how much money I could cough up (a percentage of which would be his). His grin was that of a used-car salesman about to unload a lemon on a rube. "I know a nice girl—kind of shy, mind you—who waits on tables downstairs. She gets off at nine and . . ."

While he was delivering his sales talk, I handed him a picture of Nicole playing poker. He admired her for a few seconds before he realized why I was showing it to him. He thrust it back into my hands, shaking his head. "Sorry. The waitress I told you about isn't in the same class as this chick. But her hair is almost the same color—"

"No," I said, holding the print by the edges. "I don't want someone that looks *like* her. I'm actually looking *for* her."

The bellhop displayed good-natured incredulity at my high standards in women. He reached in his pocket to return his tip, but I waved him off. He didn't need any more coaxing than that. "I'm sorry," he said. "She's way out of my league. I don't know *any* women who look that good, let alone one I can arrange a date with. Hell, if I did, I'd never make any money. I'd be taking it all out in trade, if you get my drift."

"Do you know someone I could call?"

"Not around here. For someone like her, you're talking out of town. *Way* out of town."

"That's what I was afraid of." As I showed the bellhop out, I heard the clonk of melted ice settling in the plastic bucket he had delivered. I looked at my watch. Fifty minutes from now the MC at the Mystic Isle would be introducing my act. Feeling listless and defeated, I slung my tuxedo over my back. For now, the sweet ladies of the evening would have to wait.

The manager of the Mystic Isle kept a two-year-old copy of the Manhattan Yellow Pages in his office. So far I had found over twenty-five escort services listed in New York City. I immediately eliminated agencies that used such words as "Hot" and "XXX" and also those that featured crude drawings in their ads.

Back in my hotel room, I called my way down the list, talking to businesses with such elegant names as Entre Nous and L'Abandon, and getting basically the same answer from each: "You're calling from where? Sir, you're too far away. The next time you're in the city, though, give us a ring. In any case, we don't have anyone named Nicole. But before you hang up, tell us more about this—heh-heh—'poker game' you want her to play. In our business, we're always interested in something new.''

It took forty-five minutes to make all the calls. I left my name and the phone number of the Spears Hotel with each escort service.

With that task out of the way, there was nothing to do but kill time. I set up a small three-way mirror on the dresser top and began practicing a new routine in which a deck of cards gradually shrinks down to one-inch-high cards. I was using pure sleight of hand—no gimmicked cards. As my fingers struggled through the moves, I figured it would be a minimum of six months before I could try it out on a paying audience. The cards seemed to have a will of their own, either flipping out of my grasp or sawing their edges into the sides of my fingers. I lost track of time, which was exactly what I was hoping for.

I kept working until my fingers felt as if they'd been dipped in boiling wax. While I was spreading skin cream on my hands, the phone rang. I heard a female voice with a sweet yet sultry lilt. ''Is this you, Harry? God, I thought there was surely a mistake. Are you really staying at the Spears Hotel?'' There was a pause. I think she shuddered with distaste. Then she said, ''I'll be right over.''

After she clicked off, I didn't hang up for several seconds. It was seldom that I heard a voice that was *born* to be carried over the phone lines, a voice that conjured up the kind of voluptuous images that made Hollywood fortunes. I thought about going and slipping the security man a few dollars to make sure he wouldn't hassle Nicole when she passed through the lobby, but I knew that wouldn't be necessary. She'd be an old hand at handling house detectives.

Although my fingers still ached, I again attacked my cards, wondering if the routine would ever be show-worthy. As I studied the triple image of my fingers in the three-way mirror, I also wondered why they were quivering so much.

CHAPTER FOURTEEN

The knock at the door was barely audible . . . a slow, insistent tapping, meant to make me shiver in anticipation—which it did.

Peering through the peephole, I was reminded of those viewers you hold to the light to see the picture of a pretty girl. Except the image of this pretty girl was anything but static. The languorous way Nicole stroked her hair with her jeweled hands, the way she widened her eyes, her provocative stance—all were calculated to make a man fumble with the lock of his hotel door. Although I managed to calmly undo the door chain, I didn't like the cool moistness on my palms.

We greeted each other politely as she sized up my room. The sparkle faded from her eyes as it became apparent the place did indeed match her worst expectations. Hotel rooms meant nothing to me except a place to sack out between shows, the cheaper the better. But for Nicole, they *were* her business. My room here at the Spears Hotel, with its wobbly furniture, flaking paint, and lack of air conditioning seemed an insult to her. She was used to far better.

Her gown was a shimmering cerise, exposing her creamy shoulders. She carried a tiny matching purse. I motioned her to sit on the chair by the window, but she ignored me and cleared space on the edge of the bed. I moved to the dresser, where I ripped the tissue covers off two glasses and poured in some whiskey of dubious quality.

As I handed Nicole her drink, my feet slipped on some playing cards. Nicole scrambled out of the way, her purse rolling off her lap. While she tried to steady her glass to keep from spilling whiskey on her dress, I rescued her purse. She seemed more relieved over saving her purse from hitting the floor than from keeping her dress from being stained. With good reason, I soon found out.

After returning her purse, I handed her the section of the newspaper with the story on Lisa South.

"No, thanks. I already read it," she said. "And by the way, Nicole isn't really my name. You can call me Nikki." Sniffing the whiskey, she jerked her head away in distaste. Then she shrugged and decided to play hit-and-run with her taste buds, taking a big gulp. Finally she said, "Yeah, I read that article. *Four times.*"

Keeping one hand behind my back, I pulled a chair close. She glanced at her watch and said, "Can you keep this brief? I have a date tonight." Then she added quickly, "A *real* date. I don't do the other kind anymore."

"Look what I found," I said, bringing out what I'd been hiding behind my back—a nickel-plated automatic pistol that I'd filched from her purse while she was balancing her drink. I dangled it on my finger, watching it catch the light like the fender of a new bicycle. It looked like a toy, but a close-range shot would make pudding of my insides. Nikki ducked. "Not to worry," I said, spreading my other hand. Perched between my fingers were the bullets I had emptied from the gun. "You can have this"—I handed back her pistol—"but I'll hold on to these." I closed my hand and clinked the bullets together. When I opened my hand, the bullets were gone.

She pointed at the news article. "You don't think that I—I *did* that, do you?"

I shook my head. "Not with this gun, anyway. The police say the murder weapon was a forty-five caliber. Yours is a twenty-five and hasn't been fired recently."

"It's *never* been fired, as a matter of fact. When I started in this business, I was terrified. My trusty little six-shooter was standard on-the-job equipment. After learning that most of my fears were unfounded, I started leaving the gun at home."

"Yet you considered it standard equipment tonight. You aren't totally convinced of *my* innocence, are you?"

"We aren't playing poker right now. There's no need to bluff. I know who you really are. You're Harry Colderwood the magician, right? The papers say you're the boyfriend of the woman accused of the murder."

''The reporters weren't quite accurate. It should have read 'former boyfriend.' ''

''To answer your question: I thought the gun *was* necessary. I had no idea why you lured me here. Maybe you want to knock me off and shift all the blame for the South murder to me.''

''Hey, I am working to clear Cate's name, but I don't want to hang the rap on another innocent person. I just want to nab the guilty one.''

She looked down at the empty glass in her hands, as if regretting having downed her drink so fast. As I built us refills, she sighed and said, ''What choice do I have now? I've got the gun, but you've got the bullets. Just another twist to my life's story. What do you want from me?''

I handed her a fresh drink, sat down, and—for the first time since she'd arrived—relaxed. ''For starters, what do you know about the poker game?''

The story she told me was identical to Milan Posar's: she got involved in the game after receiving an invitation in the mail. What differed was her motive for playing. ''As you could tell from the other night, I'm not a crackerjack card player. To understand what attracted me to the game, you have to know a few things about me. I started out in the escort business as just another working girl. During the day I had a nowhere job, cooped up in an office full of cubicles with thirty-five other women just as bored as me. But I was the only one who did anything about it. No, I take that back. I was one of only *two* girls who did anything about it. Noticing that one of my best friends at the office always had plenty of money, I asked her what her secret was. She told me about a great way to supplement my income *and* beat the boredom of my job. To make a long story short, I found out she wasn't selling Tupperware.'' Her sudden smile took my breath away. ''You know, I have a lot of different answers to the question: *How did a girl like you get started in this work?* But you're the first man I've ever been straight with. You should feel special, Harry.''

But my cynical nature wouldn't allow that. After all, I thought, part of her job is to make her customers feel special. However, as she continued talking, she made me forget, like any good storyteller does, that I was listening to mere words. I could clearly see the mental pictures she was creating. Perhaps this was a skill she had learned indirectly from her profession.

Nikki earned over thirty thousand tax-free dollars her first year with the escort service, working only two or three nights a week. During that time, she became fascinated with the business. Because her contralto voice was even more sexy than her body, she began to work extra hours, answering the phones. She loved selecting the right woman to match each client's fantasy. It was like playing a board game with real people. Realizing Nikki's special talent, the owner offered her a raise to handle the phones and not go out on dates anymore. That lasted two years, until the owner went to prison on a cocaine conviction. Nikki then bought the agency from him and revamped the operation, working aggressively to attract new clients. Finding out that she had a good business head, she doubled the cash flow in a short time. Nikki's "dating" days were over for good.

"That was five years ago and I've never looked back," she said. She was holding her drink stiffly now, having lost interest in it. "It wasn't until last year that I began to realize the toll my business was taking on me. Oh, the obvious fears gnawed at me. I was paranoid about the police, imagining that every new client was an undercover cop. And, of course, there were the worries of a hostile takeover . . . and I don't mean from a *Fortune* 500 company. I mean the big boys, the ones who show up at night with gasoline-soaked rags and baseball bats if you don't play ball with them. It's no wonder I developed ulcers. Not to mention a tendency to finish every drink I start and refill every one I finish. But my biggest problem was social, not economic. I let my personal life slip away. My usual routine was to work all night, sleep past noon, and then head back to the agency to start over again. Seven days a week of that makes for a lonely existence. It's damn near impossible to find someone who wants to go out on a 'normal' date at three in the afternoon."

"With all that to contend with, what brings you to Parrish?"

"It's part of my grand plan to gradually separate myself from the business. A few months ago, I started grooming one of my assistants to run the day-to-day operations. I scouted around for a small, pleasant town, close enough to the city so I could make it back quickly in case of an emergency. I rented a house here in Parrish and have been staying for increasingly longer periods. But it's hard to cut myself off totally from all the action. That's why I carry a pocket pager. A local answering service can beep me if there's a crisis my assistant can't handle."

Nikki searched through her purse, and for a moment I feared she would pull out a weapon I'd missed. Instead of a gun, she took out a strip of torn newspaper and set it aside without looking at it. I said, "Your assistant paged you tonight after I talked with her, right?"

Nikki nodded. "Yeah. You set off a four-bell alarm in her head—I never use my real name in connection with the business. When I'm on the phone with customers, I call myself Monica. When you called, asking for Nicole—which is close to Nikki—my assistant thought I was in trouble. Or that you were a cop harassing us. When she told me your name was Harry and that you mentioned a poker game, I knew it was you."

"Speaking of the game, you still haven't said what attracted you to it. All I know is, judging by your playing skill, you weren't there for the money."

She smiled wryly. "Was I that bad? Gee, I thought I faked it fairly well. You know, I wasn't even sure of all the rules when I got that invitation. The last time I'd played poker was as a girl at camp. Would you believe I actually went out and bought a book on how to play? For practice, I pumped a lot of money into a video poker game in a local pub."

"But why—?"

"As I said, the last five years have been a constant treadmill of work. I've gotten out of practice in most social situations—*normal* social situations, that is. Unless I have a phone in my hand and am talking sweet and seductively to a wealthy man in heat, I feel lost. Even though it was expensive—$15,000 a pop—the poker game seemed like an ideal way to start easing back. Its structure was perfect for me."

"I don't understand."

"First of all, the secrecy of it . . . being prohibited to use our real names, and to talk about our private lives. Second, the chance of losing money made it exciting. And yet at the same time it was all quite safe and controlled."

I nodded. "And it reminded you in some ways of your own business."

"You hit it. Fictitious names, lies about our personal lives, plenty of money changing hands, entertainment without the risk of personal involvement . . ."

"Plus, there was someone unseen in the background, pulling

the strings, just as you do for your escort service. Do you have any idea who's behind the poker game?''

She looked at me thoughtfully and shook her head. ''There's no way of knowing if it's one of the players. But I am sure it's tied up with *this.*'' She laid her news clipping on my lap. It was another article about the murder, this one from a Philadelphia paper. ''It says Lisa South was killed during the same time we were playing cards.''

''So what?'' I said. ''Even in a town this small, all sorts of crimes were probably committed during that period.''

''But no crimes that I had a motive for.''

Sadness settled over her face and the corners of her eyes glistened. I couldn't tell if her emotion was genuine or not.

''You knew Lisa South?'' I asked.

''Not personally. I started reading her column when I found out she had a summer home in Parrish. In a way I envied her. At least she could be open about what she did for a living. Lately, Lisa had been getting acclaim because her columns were venturing away from pure gossip and into investigative journalism. In one of her columns a month ago, she promised an upcoming series on 'working girls,' even though, she said, she'd found out she wasn't the 'type,' that she couldn't make the 'cut.' ''

''What does that mean?''

''I'm sure she was referring to my escort service. While other agencies hire solely on appearance, I actually conduct interviews, just like a regular business. Although our ads in local magazines are discreet, the response is overwhelming. I preface each interview by explaining how few girls are the right type, how few will make the cut. After seeing Lisa South use the words 'cut' and 'type,' I looked through my files and found this.'' She handed me a snapshot from her purse. The woman in the picture wore a bleach-white wig. She seemed uncomfortable in her tight leather jacket. Her heavy pink lipstick and blue eye shadow were applied with too much calculation. She vaguely resembled Lisa South.

Nikki said, ''I interviewed this woman eight weeks ago. She said her name was Liza Sauter.''

''You turned her down?''

She laughed. ''Of course. Look at her. You wouldn't believe how many of her type we get. She dressed like a streetwalker, not stopping to think that we charge two hundred an hour and don't want our girls to look like a trashy stereotype. My girls dress like business women going out for a night on the town. That's why they're never stopped by hotel security. I can't recall every detail of Lisa South's interview, but I do remember she put on quite an act, talking tough and tossing off plenty of vulgar words. She failed to understand that I want my girls to create the illusion of a casual date that ends in seduction rather than to act like a hooker who is punching an expensive time clock.''

''Did she bring this picture with her?''

''No, I photograph everyone I interview. They help us decide whom to call back for a follow-up. The pictures also aid in describing our girls to clients over the phone.''

''How long did the interview last?''

''My attached notes were brief, so I'd guess maybe ten minutes.''

''What harm could she do in so short a time?''

''Plenty. Two days after her interview, my office was broken into.''

''Anything missing?''

''No. Which isn't to say that nothing was stolen.''

''How do you mean?'' I snapped my fingers and a cigarette appeared between them. Its coal glowed mightily on my first puff. Cigarettes always taste better when I get them this way. I offered Nikki one and she shook her head.

She squinted at me through the smoky haze and waved the photo. ''Let's just say that I had something of hers. And she had something of mine.''

I nodded with understanding. ''I see. You think she cased your office during the interview, and later rifled it and copied your client list, right?''

''Yep. I should have seen it coming. Ever since South did those profiles on leaders in the women's movement, her writing has leaned more toward feminist issues. Occasionally she spoke out on issues of pornography and prostitution. There were a lot of big names on my list, highly visible men in sensitive positions—the kind who love getting their names in the paper, but not for their extracurricular activities.''

''But aren't you just speculating? Nothing was missing.''

''I phoned Lisa several times, but she never returned my calls. I finally got through last weekend and asked her point-blank about my client list. She refused to talk about it but did make an appointment to meet me ''

"At her house?"

"No, her office."

"And where's that?"

"She keeps a small one here in town. On the twenty-four-hundred block of O'Malley Street on the fourth floor. Our meeting would have been tonight. During our phone conversation, she played it close to the vest, never admitting about coming in disguise for an interview.'' She shook her head sadly. *"She should have been the one playing poker with us. Well, at least that card game gives me an alibi."*

"Unfortunately, Nikki, it's no good. No one in our little poker league has an alibi.'' I explained how one of the players had slipped out the bathroom window.

With a gleam in her eye, she said, "This could be the first time I've been accused of fleeing through a bathroom window when I'm completely innocent.'' Her expression sobered when I took a final drag and ground my cigarette out in my palm, showing no pain. "Wow," she said, "you really are serious about finding out who's behind this, aren't you? Sorry, I haven't a clue."

As she stood to leave, I said, "What about the other two players, Les and John? Do you know who they are?"

Nikki appeared to mull over the question, but I was certain she knew more than she was telling. Like a kid caught pulling a prank, she wouldn't want to take all the blame. She was debating upon which man to save as a future bargaining chip. Finally, she said, "I did get some impressions about John. For one thing, I'm sure he doesn't have a regular job. In my business, you get good at reading people. You learn to smell deadbeats a mile away. Also, I didn't like the way he treated me. No matter what I did—wink, smile, try to strike up a conversation—he paid no attention to me. I was just another guy in the game—nothing more than a stack of chips to win."

"Do you think he's gay?"

"No, I just think that sex isn't as important to him as other things. When a guy like him has gambling on his mind, I doubt if even my best girl could get a rise out of him."

"You think he's a compulsive gambler?"

She nodded.

"Do you think he lives around here?"

"Definitely not," she said. "This town isn't fast enough for John's gaming appetite. As a matter of fact, the day before yesterday I was picking up an express package at the Greyhound Terminal. And whom do I see stepping off a bus, but John? I turned my head so he wouldn't spot me."

"Where was he coming from?"

"His bus said Atlantic City, and I can't say I was too surprised."

I thanked her for her help. As I watched her head for the door, I dreaded the silence that would soon surround me. The room felt small and cold, and Nikki's company seemed suddenly desirable. "Nikki, you don't really have a date tonight, do you?"

Her smile was practiced, concealing her real feelings. It was a smile that used to earn her living, a smile that said I was the most important man in the world to her. But then a trace of sadness came over her face and she said, "No, I lied. But Harry, I'm not really looking for a date. Before you even ask the question, my answer is no thanks." She pursed her lips. "I guess I've gotten too good at reading people."

"Oh yeah? And how do you read me?"

Nikki sighed. "Regardless of what's going through your mind right now, the truth is you aren't really interested in me. You feel the walls closing in . . . and think that my companionship will ease your mind. Maybe you're afraid that you've bitten off too much with this case. Well, Harry, don't worry about the walls. They've threatened to close in on me lately, too. But they haven't, so far, and there's no reason they will on you." She paused and looked at me with something like longing in her eyes. "Your friend Cate must be real special for you to go through all this. Here's my number if you need to call. And by the way, I never told you my last name. It's Beacham." She wrote her number on a slip of paper and handed it to me.

As the door closed behind her a jumble of words flashed through my mind: *girls, business, clients, appointments, dates, escort service.* Euphemisms. Nikki Beacham was quite adept at using them. I stood in front of the mirror and began practicing my diminishing cards again, fighting off the shivers that Nikki said she'd learned to live with. More euphemisms zapped through my head: *magic man, conjuror, prestidigitator, sleight-of-hand man, wizard.* My fingers stiffened and the cards were hard to hold.

I walked closer to the mirror and stared at the person who tomorrow night would again cavort around the stage of the Mystic Isle, performing the impossible with cards, handkerchiefs, and pretty little balls. My mind gradually focused on one word, which was not a euphemism. I said it aloud: "Charlatan."

The word didn't sting as badly as I'd feared.

John could dream of royal flushes, running the crap table, and breaking the bank at baccarat. What kept me going was my obsession with fooling people. Whoever had engineered the kidnapping of Cate, the poker game with inflated stakes, and the murder of Lisa South was muscling in on my territory. He was trying to fool everyone—trying to fool *me*. And I didn't like it. No real magician would.

I vowed to use every grubby trick in my charlatan's book to get to the bottom of it. I gathered my cards up off the floor, squared them, and ran through the routine again. This time the roughness was gone. My fingers felt nimble and loose. The moves were flawless. The routine *looked* like magic again.

During my fifteenth run-through, my fingers tingling with pain, I came up with a way to locate John.

Aha, I thought. You *can* teach an old charlatan new tricks.

CHAPTER FIFTEEN

Several years ago, Al Emmons, owner of the Mystic Isle, printed up an advertising brochure. It include full-color photos of the club and the various acts that had played there, including Blackstone, Copperfield, and Henning. (There was even a small photo of a young magician named Colderwood.) The picture of the basement on the last page always made me chuckle. For the purposes of the brochure, Emmons had transformed the dark, dank cellar into a combination medieval street fair and Santa's workshop. Spicing up the photo were a half-dozen magicians rehearsing in full costume. In the background, carpenters busily hammered on magic illusions. In reality, the basement was little more than a dressing room area. The illusions in the picture had been carted over from the warehouse next door where Emmons stored his vast collection of magic apparatus.

Sitting inside my dressing room, I looked out at the main room of the basement and saw little similarity to Emmons's photo version. The room was long and narrow, with brick walls and a crumbling cement floor. Dressing room doors lined the walls on either side. On the ceiling, directly above a pile of mattresses on the floor, was a trap door, used as often by performers at this club as a regular stage door was at a legitimate theatre. In the center of the room was a makeshift lounge, furnished with old chairs and sofas that raised dust if you sat down too hard. A steep, rubber-treaded stairway at the far end led up to the back-stage area. Next to the stairway stood a freight elevator, its doors operated by an ancient rope-and-pulley system. The elevator was used for transporting illusions and other equipment to the stage. On the opposite wall was a pair of dungeon-like steel doors secured by a two-by-six plank that could have withstood a battering ram. On the other side of the doors lay a tunnel leading to Emmons's warehouse. Emmons still had plenty of space in his warehouse and had repeatedly asked me to sell him my old illusion show, which was now in mothballs out on the Coast. Even though I hadn't used the equipment in years, there was something reassuring about holding on to it.

The dressing rooms in the Mystic Isle were cramped little alcoves, with wooden benches that faced walls of smudged mirrors. The mirrors were bordered by big light bulbs that made each room feel like an incubator. To keep the performers from missing their cues, each dressing room was equipped with a wall-mounted speaker that piped in the sounds of the act currently playing. There was no Off switch. One of the dressing rooms even had a TV monitor showing what was going on up onstage.

The only private dressing room in the club was at the far end of the basement. Instead of a star, the door was decorated with a silver cutout of a top hat. This room was air-conditioned and included a private shower, a small refrigerator, and a telephone. When I last played the Mystic Isle—years ago—Al Emmons had insisted that I take the Top Hat room. But this time, the room was locked up tight. No stars were playing the club this week.

On the wall beside the Top Hat room hung a portrait of Griffin Page, the first big-name magician to play the Mystic Isle. The photo had been taken in Page's waning years. His handsome brown eyes were obscured by thick glasses and he looked like an authoritative grandfather watching over his progeny.

I was now listening to the closing music of the Great Wylini. His music was mostly novelty stuff—plenty of bells, horns, and raspberry noises. Wylini's entire act consisted of audience volunteers sitting down on folding chairs. The results were hilarious as their seats gradually became too hot to sit on.

As the music for the next act started—a dreamy Strauss waltz that floated out of the speaker and seemed to stagnate and decay in midair—I wiped the rest of the cold cream from my face with a theatrical napkin. I could picture in my mind each trick that the magician on stage was now performing. The magician, a nineteen-year-old who billed himself simply as "Edward," had choreographed his act perfectly to his music—note for note, step for step. Each performance was a carbon copy of the last. Edward never divulged his last name, but he once admitted that he detested being called Eddie. Naturally I called him Eddie thereafter. Edward's act consisted of magically producing gaily painted Oriental parasols—so many that the stage crew needed several minutes to clear the stage at the end of his performance.

At the final timpani roll of Edward's music, I threw away my napkin and turned to watch the two magicians behind me. They were both straddling a bench, facing each other. Barely in their twenties, they both wore flowered polyester shirts that hung from their spindly arms like loose skin. Their blond hair was identically styled: parted in the middle, swept back behind the ears, and cascading down the backs of their necks in corkscrew curls. They billed themselves as the Dean Brothers, and they performed a synchronized sleight of hand act with doves, ropes, and ribbons. They worked so well together that most audiences assumed they were brothers, but—as was often the case with show-biz "brothers"—they weren't related. Their close rapport was a result of endless practice since the age of ten as they grew up in the same neighborhood. Their obsession with creating the perfect pantomime act allowed little time for growth in other areas, and in many ways they were still ten-year-old boys. Not having changed their act significantly in five years, they were like gymnasts trying to turn a 9.99 into a perfect 10.

Edward and the Dean Brothers usually avoided talking to me. They treated me like a royal family member who had abdicated. I suspected that they couldn't forgive me for chucking away the brass ring of stardom they were all killing themselves to reach.

The Dean Brothers, having already performed their act, were arguing over the best way to force the choice of a playing card. The brother on the right said, "The slip force is the best. Never fails. Once you got it down cold, nothing can go wrong."

"It's a waste of time," the other Dean said. "The classic force is the only one worth learning. It's the most natural."

"But it's not a hundred-percent reliable. If the volunteer moves his hand a fraction at the wrong time, he's going to miss the card you're trying to fob off on him. That constant worry takes the edge off your performance."

As I started to leave the dressing room, the first Dean said, "Here," and shoved a deck of cards at me. For the eighty-thousandth time in my life, someone wanted me to "pick-a-card-any-card" . . . the prelude to some of the finest—but often the most boring—tricks in magic.

My reflexes overruled my better judgment, and I slid a card from his neat fan. I looked at it and returned it. "Ace of Hearts, right?" he said. I nodded and tried to walk around him. He thrust the deck at me again, this time close to my face. I sighed and selected another. The Ace of Hearts again. I sidled away from him toward the door, but he mirrored my every step, holding the deck under my nose as a mugger would a knife.

"Help," I said in mock dismay. "Somebody, please." But the Mystic Isle was the last place in the world I could expect to be rescued from an out-of-control magician. I succumbed and picked again. It was—what else?—the Ace of Hearts. I was almost at the door when I saw the deck zooming toward me again from the right. I feigned with my left and parried with my right, blocking his wrist and wresting the cards from him. I slapped the deck down on the bench in front of the second Dean and said, "I'll settle the argument. Why don't *you* pick a card?" I spread the deck and mixed it around until it was a mess of random cards. "That's the last time I'll touch them." The Dean brother's finger hovered indecisively before touching the corner of one card. "Four of Clubs," I announced.

He shrugged and turned the card over to show his partner I was right. I said, "Put it back and mix them. Yeah, that's it. Swirl them around until you've lost track of your card. Now pick again. Notice I haven't gone near the deck." The card he turned over was again the Four of Clubs.

"Try it again," I said. And again he chose the Four of Clubs. Now I had their attention.

The other Dean stroked his chin, exposing a set of buffed fingernails that sparkled as brilliantly as his capped teeth. He was staring at the cards as though there might be instructions on them revealing how I was able to force a card without touching the deck. "Brother," he said to his partner, "I think he originally spread these cards in a subtle pattern that makes you subconsciously choose the same card each time, even after shuffling them."

The second Dean hated this explanation. He picked another card, which he quickly slapped down without showing. His frown told me that it was the Four of Clubs. He scrambled the cards with both hands for several seconds, hesitating before choosing again. His confidence was shaken. He reminded me of a schoolyard bully finally facing an opponent who'd taken boxing lessons.

I laid a comforting hand on the shoulder of the second Dean. "You might call yours the Classic Force, but mine's the *genuine* classic. I learned it when I was seven, but it never fooled my friends. They laughed so hard, I almost gave up magic. Funny, but years later I discovered that for some reason this force *always* fools magicians. Maybe you and your brother should get out into the real world more often."

On my way out, he chose another card. Of course it was again the Four of Clubs. He squeezed the edge so hard his thumbnail turned red.

Out in the main room of the basement, I passed a morose Edward. He was carrying a spiral notebook and a Styrofoam cooler with a strap. Wearing an immaculate, perfectly tailored black tuxedo, he was one magician who would never be mistaken for a maitre d' or a prom date. A short young man of nineteen who brooked no wisecracks about his height, Edward had the face of an accountant and the hands of a surgeon. I nodded to him, but he ignored me and walked briskly to the corner dressing room where each night he anxiously scrutinized the videotape of his parasol act. Freezing each frame, he dissected his routine move by move, always searching for flaws. I once asked Edward if he would ever consider working with props other than little umbrellas, and he said he was developing a routine with gold coins—which he'd be ready to try out in eight years.

Standing in the doorway of his dressing room, I watched him pop his tape into the VCR. The monitor above the tape machine showed a live close-up of the master of ceremonies doing a trick with a twenty-dollar bill borrowed from an audience member. The camera zeroed in on the redheaded man who had lent the bill. With his red cowlick dancing in the back and his sport coat with patched sleeves, he looked oddly familiar. As the camera followed him back to his seat, I moved closer to the monitor. I was right—whispering in a waiter's ear was Buzz Kerns, Cate's lawyer. I watched Kerns get up and hurry toward the backstage area, leaving behind his twenty-dollar bill for the MC to work his magic on. If Kerns headed directly downstairs, I'd never make it out of the club without passing him. I didn't know what he wanted, but any delay could ruin my plans for tonight. Tired of having me hog his screen, Edward hit the Play button. The pic-

ture of the MC ripping up Kerns's bill was replaced by Edward
plucking lacy parasols from the air.

I looked out into the main room of the basement, at the double
metal doors with the bar across them. "Eddie—I mean Edward—
I truly enjoy the work of you younger guys. Every night I'm
glued to this monitor, marveling at how you do exactly the same
thing show after show, year after year . . . like human Xerox
machines. Now, I don't mean to intrude—I know *I* hate unsoli-
cited criticism—but lately I've noticed that you've been flashing
your final big load, that six-foot-wide parasol."

Horror lived in his eyes, as though I were a doctor informing
him of a dreaded disease. I said, "If you don't believe me, check
out your tape. But don't worry, I know how to fix the problem.
Of course, who am I to give advice? My act is an old-fashioned
repertoire of sleights, pantomime, jokes, illusions, escapes—the
whole gamut. What do I know about high-powered pure sleight
of hand?" I turned to leave and he grabbed my sleeve, nearly
ripping it. "Do you really want my advice?"

He nodded vigorously, nearly mussing his pompadour. "Edward, I'll gladly help, but I need a favor. I'm in a bind. In a few
minutes a guy with red hair will show up here, asking odd questions about me. Any way you could waylay him? I don't want to
be followed."

Edward drew a can of Diet Dr Pepper from his Styrofoam
cooler, pulled the tab, and slid in a straw. The liquid swept up
and down the straw as he took a thoughtful swallow. He finally
nodded and jabbed the Forward Scan button on the VCR. His
image jitterbugged across the screen, filling the stage with parasols. Taking another sip of Dr Pepper, he poked the Freeze-
Frame button at the point in his routine when he was about to
produce his giant umbrella. He laid a fingertip on the screen,
touching the inside of his tux coat. He looked at me with wide,
sad eyes.

"Yeah. That's it," I said. "Under your right arm. Your load is
visible from that side of the audience. The way I see it, if you
rotate ten degrees counterclockwise, it'll cover your move."

Edward opened his notebook to a clean page, uncapped a
roller-point pen, and—oblivious to my fidgeting—began printing
notes. After recapping his pen, he walked a few steps out of his
dressing room and pivoted his head from left to right, trying to
decide where to hide me.

He pointed in the direction of the Top Hat dressing room. I smiled wistfully and said, "No, I won't use that room again until I'm officially invited. Besides, I can't afford to hole up in there for hours, my ear pressed to the door, wondering if the coast is clear."

He went over to the freight elevator and pulled the rope to open the doors. They wouldn't budge, meaning that the crew upstairs was loading something onboard. As he enjoyed more of his Dr Pepper, his eyes wandered around the room until they settled on the barred double doors. His face lit up. I had never seen Edward smile before. The gap between his two front teeth startled me.

"The tunnel," I said. "Splendid idea."

Keeping his straw a constant inch away from his lips, Edward followed me over to the doors. As I passed the Dean Brothers' dressing room, I heard them arguing over who got first dibs at punching me in the jaw. I took it they'd figured out my "innovative" force.

"Don't tell the Dean Brothers where I went, either," I said in a low voice.

Imitating a weight lifter, I positioned myself under the board across the double doors and lifted and grunted. On my second try I hoisted it up and away. After taking a shaky step to keep my balance, I eased it to the floor without a sound. Bracing my foot against the left door, I grabbed the handle on the right door and yanked it open. Cool, damp air rolled out of the passage with an odor reminiscent of wet laundry. Light from the basement illuminated the first few feet of the tunnel, and I could see that the cracked cement floor was dotted with puddles. The stone walls glistened with moisture and thick cobwebs masked many of the crannies. I took a few hesitant steps and turned to thank Edward. Before I could speak, he slammed the doors shut and dropped the plank into place. For a second, in the pitch blackness, I imagined Edward laughingly telling the Dean Brothers about how he tricked me into the tunnel. I visualized the trio racing next door to the warehouse to nail shut the exit at the other end of the tunnel. But my fears vanished when I heard the Dean Brothers outside the tunnel doors, still cursing me out. They asked where I was and Edward said he didn't know.

I dragged my fingers along the walls, shaking away spider webs, until I located a light switch. I decided to hold off flicking it, fearing that light would seep through the cracks under the doors. I heard a tick-ticking on the floor and stiffened. Something furry brushed my ankle. I kicked hard and the tick-ticking retreated. Flattening my ear to the door, I caught snatches of conversation from the other side.

The first voice was Buzz Kerns's. As he tried to wheedle information about my whereabouts, I imagined Edward staring him down, calmly enjoying the hell out of his Dr Pepper. Finally giving up, Kerns gave Edward a message for me: "Tell Harry I hired a handwriting expert with court experience who is going to work up a psychological profile of the kidnapper, based on the note."

Edward said something unintelligible and Kerns replied, "What do you mean graphology isn't scientific? It's what? Now wait, that's going too far, buddy. Handwriting analysts are *not* in the same league as aluminum-siding men who rip off old people. When you see Harry, just tell him that I—"

Kerns's voice faded in the direction of the stairway, and I heard the Dean Brothers still arguing bitterly. They were blaming each other for letting me switch their deck of cards for one with fifty-two Fours of Clubs. As their voices drifted off, I switched on the light and began my trek along the tunnel. At the other end, I stopped in front of another set of double doors. There was no board on these doors, just a dead-bolt lock. At first the lock fiercely resisted my set of picks, losing three minutes later.

I switched off the tunnel lights, relocked the doors behind me, and turned to gaze upon a huge room that seemed to have sprung from my wildest childhood dreams—rows upon rows of brightly painted boxes and tables and cages and swords. Stacked along the wall were crates with such tantalizing labels as Egyptian Sawing in Half, Torches Through the Lady, and The Triple Cremation. This lowest level of the three-story warehouse contained the lion's share of Emmons's illusion collection, one of the largest in the East. Emmons maintained this stock of magic partly as an expensive hobby and partly for the convenience of big-name conjurors who occasionally dropped by the club unannounced. Emmons also rented out equipment to corporations that wanted a touch of magic for sales meetings and trade shows.

I wandered into the workshop at the far corner of the warehouse and was surprised at the number of illusions being refurbished. I figured this to be the work of Ed McClenahan, the newest stagehand at the club. McClenahan had a reputation as an imaginative creator of finely detailed sets and props.

Resisting the urge to paw through the goodies in this treasure house, I moved toward the exit. It was eleven o'clock. I calculated that the poker player named John had probably been awake for only two hours.

I had until dawn to locate him.

CHAPTER SIXTEEN

I found John hunkered down in the back room of a gas station, looking hollow-cheeked and bleary-eyed. He was wearing the same shirt as when I'd last seen him, and his hair needed combing. He and four other men were tossing dice and wailing like a revival meeting congregation. Drowning out the click of the dice was the whir of an air wrench as a midnight mechanic threw on a set of tires. The gas station was long closed, but the back room was only now getting warmed up.

I had started out the evening asking questions at the bus station, checking out the late-night action in town. This was the third game I had crashed. The first two were card games in which I played a few losing hands before remembering another "appointment" and gracefully waltzing away. If the action had been heavier in Parrish tonight, it might have taken until dawn to catch up to John.

It was now John's turn to roll. His pile of money was the lowest of the players. He cupped the dice in his hands and blew on them, then he flung the white cubes across the floor. They ended up snake eyes, mocking his efforts to influence them.

As the man next to him snatched up the dice, John's eyes met mine. He looked stunned, as though someone had backhanded him across the face. He didn't know why I was here, only that I wasn't about to help him.

The man nearest me wore a denim shirt with an oil company insignia on the pocket. A tie tack, also with the company logo, held his neatly knotted tie in place. All the crapshooters—except John—greeted me with the same wolfish grin. "Welcome, stranger," the man in the tie said. "Come to give us all your money?"

As a matter of fact, I have, I thought, squeezing into the circle of players. My strategy was to lose a few times, mutter about a bad-luck streak, and then quietly clear out . . . taking John with me.

John had three losing rolls of the dice before he realized what I was doing. "Hey," the man in the tie said to me, "you not only have crummy luck, but it's rubbing off on John too." John cursed at the dice. For the first time in his crapshooting career, John was right—the dice *were* to blame for him losing. Each time it was his turn, I switched the dice for a pair that would roll only boxcars and snake eyes. After he crapped out, I switched the genuine pair back in.

Even though I encouraged John to keep playing, when his fourth roll ended in disaster he got up and hurried out of the gas station without a word. I followed, commenting that he looked ill. The man in the necktie told me to hurry back, that he liked my style. I didn't blame him, considering that I had dumped two hundred dollars into the game in the last three minutes.

Outside, John was leaning against the blue and white tile wall next to the men's room. He lit a plastic-tipped cigar and looked up at the clouds that were drifting past the quarter moon. I could barely hear the cheers of the dice players as they continued to empty and fill each other's pockets.

John regarded me with the pained expression of a dog trying to shake free of burrs. "Who the hell are you?" he said. He took a puff and exhaled a hissing cloud of smoke. "Christ, you even make my cigars taste bad. Damn you, that poker game the other night was *my* game. I finally had Miles figured out and was sure I'd win big. Then you show up out of nowhere and shut us all down. I didn't even have enough bread to haul ass out of this backwater town. So tonight—just when I'm getting rolling, building up a stake for the next big poker game—what happens? You show up again. What do you want?"

"Sorry I wrecked your game in there, John, but I need to talk to you. I didn't want to wait all night to get you alone. You weren't going to win tonight anyway; your strategy was all wrong. You were multiplying your bets by two every time you lost so that even a short run of losses would have spelled the end for you. It wouldn't have been long before you'd be out here anyway, leaning against the wall, smoking and looking at the moon, wondering why you were born so unlucky. All I did was save you time."

John slowly slid his glasses up his nose. He gazed at me with a look of wry amazement. "Pardon my staring, but I never thought you'd be this young. With the kind of life I've led, I've been looking over my shoulder for you for a long time. Where the hell were you three years ago when I went ice-cold at the blackjack table in Reno? Where were you when I spent sixty days in the army stockade after getting into a knife fight with a loan shark? Where were you last year when I missed the state lottery by one stinking number? And now, you son of a bitch, you finally show up when I don't need you. It's only a matter of time before I begin cashing in on that weekly poker game. But since you're standing here, I suppose I'd be foolish to pass up the opportunity. Okay, where do I sign?"

"Sign what?"

"The contract. What do you think I'm talking about?"

"What contract?"

"The one that entitles you to my soul, of course . . . while in return I get an eternity of royal flushes, winning Lotto numbers, and slot machine buckets full of silver dollars."

The clouds now blocked the moon, and his pallid cheeks and the whites of his eyes made his face look ghostly. The sky blinked brightly and there was a tremor of thunder.

I held up my hands in surrender. "Don't worry. I don't have any contract. Even though I've had a few managers I swore worked for Satan himself, I'm not the guy you want. I just want to talk to you. Why don't we get a bite to eat?"

"Okay," he said without enthusiasm.

"You'll have to buy. I'm busted. You're an expensive person to find."

I blinked my eyes twice, and two burning cigarettes appeared between my middle and first fingers. I said, "Since you've lost your taste for cigars, try one of these."

He held one of the cigarettes cautiously under his nose, making sure it was real. "Man, I can't believe this. I'm surprised that you eat real food, just like everyone else."

I sighed and said, "Right now, I'd settle for some real answers to real questions."

There were only a few all-night restaurants in Parrish. We settled on the Jolly Roger, a diner that catered to drinkers who had closed down the local bars. Obviously a frequent patron,

John led me straight to the main counter without waiting to be seated. We sat hunched forward on our stools, talking loudly to be heard over the churning milkshake machines and the whistling busboy. The two A.M. rush had not yet started.

As we ate, John told me that his real name was Jack Sullivan and that he mostly worked out of Atlantic City. He gave me an address where I could leave messages for him, but I suspected that he lived on the streets of Atlantic City.

While waiting for the waitress to refill my Coke, I took out a deck of cards and showed Sullivan a few gambling tricks, including how to use the reflection in a cup of coffee to read cards as they're dealt. I warned him not to use these tricks to cheat people, but that was as silly as putting a *For Educational Purposes* label on pornography.

"Still think I'm an agent of the devil?" I asked. Sullivan crinkled his brow but didn't answer. I said, "Maybe the devil's already contacted us."

"How's that?" he said.

"Maybe he invited us to play a little poker the other night. Why don't you tell me how you got involved?"

Sullivan was eager to talk about the big game. "Sure, I was a little curious about why I was invited, but when you've been gambling as long as me, you learn not to ask dumb questions when someone has money burning a hole in his pocket. Once I was in a bar in New Jersey and a decent-looking guy, dressed too nice for the joint, came up and offered me a hundred dollars to go to a party. I said sure. When I got there, I found there was nothing to eat or drink at this party. What this guy did was pay me and six other guys to watch him and his old lady fool around in the bedroom. One of my friends felt real bad, and he spent the rest of the night trying to figure out why a man would do such a weird thing. Me, I didn't waste time worrying. I took that hundred dollars to the track and parlayed it into three grand. When it comes to a windfall, *any* question is a stupid question."

Sullivan told me that a couple weeks ago he woke up after a three-day drunk and found an invitation to the poker game stuffed in his shirt pocket. Having been on a cold streak lately, he said he raised the requisite "entry fee" for the game by calling in markers from friends. I suspected he had actually borrowed it from some people in Atlantic City who would react most violently if he ever showed his face in town again without his pockets full of cash. "It gets harder each week to raise the jack. But, Harry, if you're going to become a regular, I'm dropping out of the game altogether."

"There won't be any more poker games, Jack." As I painted my French fries with ketchup, I told him about the Lisa South murder and its connection to the game. I told him about the open window in the bathroom.

When I finished, he said, "Lisa South? You say she was a newspaper columnist? Never heard of her. I only read the sports page and *The Racing Form*. Anyway, why would I want to kill someone like her?" He tilted his head back and finished his coffee. "What about the other poker players? Did you find any of them?"

"Les is the only one left to track down. Have any idea who he is?"

Sullivan shook his head. "Sorry. Like I said, I didn't get too curious about the setup. When I was a kid, one of my favorite stories was about the magic goose and the greedy suckers who slit it open to get all the gold. I vowed that if I ever found a goose whose eggs sparkled even a little, I'd treat it like a king."

As the waitress brought Sullivan his fourth cup of coffee, I noticed that he had eaten only a few bites of his hot roast beef sandwich. He looked so sickly and run-down that if I'd had vitamins with me, I'd have slipped them into his drink.

He bummed another cigarette from me, joking that since the price was right, he'd acquired a taste for them. Looking at his reflection in the mirror behind the counter, he shook his head sadly. "Harry, there's no reason to suspect me. I just got mixed up in something over my head. Like I said, I never heard of Lisa South, and as for the others, I don't give a damn about their identities. I was in that game for one reason—money." He asked for another cigarette. I gave him three and he slipped them into his shirt pocket. "Will you excuse me a minute? Too much coffee." He pushed his cup away and walked to the end of the counter and down a hallway to the rest room. Hands stuffed loosely in his jacket pockets, he shambled along as if time were something that only other people worried about.

I listened to the waitresses shout to the paper-hatted cooks for *bay-cod*, *fishy-may*, and *fry-o's*. As I finished my club sandwich, I eyed Sullivan's fortress-sized sandwich. The gravy had congealed and it was doomed to the scrapings of the busboy. I thought of what Nikki had said about the only appetite that ruled Sullivan's life.

As I waited, the jukebox served up another glum ballad. Someone with a pocketful of quarters had been playing an endless string of hard-luck country songs about adultery, alcoholism, and bankruptcy. Hoping to counteract the dark mood descending over the diner, I pumped in four quarters' worth of saccharine dance music. But the record machine played its music first come, first served, and the songs remained bleak.

The atmosphere didn't improve any when two beefy uniformed cops, wearing big-handled guns, swaggered into the diner and sat down next to me. Their squawking walkie-talkies provided me with a stereophonic version of the evening's troubles in Parrish. Another tearjerker limped out of the jukebox, this one about a man who loved his wife so much, he hardly ever hit her. When the song ended and Sullivan still hadn't returned, I decided to investigate.

I found the men's room empty. The window was open just wide enough for the skinny Sullivan to squeeze through. The breeze gently rippled the strip of paper towel hanging from the wall dispenser. I crawled up on the radiator below the window and looked out into an alley where a steady drizzle was making plinking sounds on rows of garbage cans.

Beautiful. Sullivan had stuck me with the dinner check. Although my wallet was loaded with credit cards, each had a "warrant" out for it. I shoved the window up as far as it would go. As the jukebox out in the diner burst forth with the first of my upbeat selections, I also heard a rasping, staticky voice. As it got louder, I recognized it as a police radio.

I stuck my head outside and looked for something to grab onto. Dance music and the cop's walkie-talkie hiss flooded the rest room as the door flew open, smashing the wall. I heard the police dispatcher alert squad cars to a fistfight at a gas station crap game.

As I wriggled outside a few inches, the policeman bellowed, "What the hell?" His fingers clamped around my ankle with a viselike grip. "Stop! Police!" I drove the heel of my other foot into his soft belly. With a whoosh of air, he released me. I heard a thump as he sat down hard on the floor and I wormed my way farther out the window. Reaching the point of no return, I still hadn't found anything to hang on to. I lost my balance and somersaulted a few feet to the ground, landing on a lumpy cushion of plastic garbage bags.

With tin cans still clanging in my ears, I lay faceup in the alley. I forced myself to get up, knowing that when the policeman caught his breath his gun would be drawn. If I didn't clear my head soon, I might end up in a plastic bag too.

I staggered to my feet and did a wobbly jog for two blocks, ducking into another alley. I stood leaning my forehead on the wall of a parking garage. I looked at my watch, wondering when the cops would lose interest in a vagrant who had helped himself to a free meal, allowing me to venture back to my van.

At this very moment, Jack Sullivan was probably scheming how to use the few hours before dawn to get back into action and rebuild his cash reserve. He said that he didn't have a motive for murdering Lisa South, but that wasn't true. He might have killed her for the same reason he weaseled out of paying for dinner—lack of money to feed his gambling habit. The artwork and jewelry missing from Lisa South's house would have been a tempting haul for a hustler like Sullivan.

I wondered if telling him about the murderer slipping out the window at the poker game had inspired him to pull tonight's stunt. Or had he been so slick in ducking out tonight because he'd already had practice?

One thing was certain—Jack Sullivan no longer thought I was supernatural. After all, you don't stiff an agent of the devil for the meal check.

CHAPTER SEVENTEEN

Screaming rubber emanated from the corner dressing room where someone was watching television. Can't be Edward, I thought. This time of day he was usually rehearsing in his motel room, trying to become the first magician in history with a totally flawless act. I stuck my head in the door and saw Mr. Memory watching TV. His bare feet propped on a bench, he clutched a bottle of Canadian Club in one hand and a glass in the other. The top three buttons of his ruffled shirt were undone and his bow tie hung from one lapel. It was two in the afternoon and I figured that he was still here from last night. I wondered if he was trying to rinse away another batch of indelible memories.

Mr. Memory gazed slack-jawed at the screen, watching stock cars tear around a dirt track. Vehicles crunched into each other exploding into flames as an announcer coldly tallied the number of injuries and deaths. The cassette package on his lap read "Fifty Greatest Racing Mishaps." Not good medicine for a morose man with a photographic memory.

"Did you find your poker buddies?" he asked.

"Three of them, thanks to you." I watched a smoking car spin toward a panicked roadside crowd at Monte Carlo. "But I still have one more to go."

"It would be a waste of time to show me those photos again. If I wanted to, I could close my eyes right now and picture them in perfect detail."

I said, "The first three poker players used names similar to their real ones; John was really Jack, Nicole was Nikki, and Miles was Milan. The one I'm still looking for is the older guy called Les." I flashed one of the photographs at him and he shielded his eyes. "I'm betting that his real name is something like Les. Maybe Leslie or Lester. Also, I got the impression from his clothes and his blasé attitude that he's wealthy. Mr. Memory, I'd like you to cull your mind and put together a list of the well-to-do men in town whose faces you've never seen and whose first names have an *l* in the beginning."

The challenge intrigued him. "You want me to include names I've seen in the news as well as those picked up in conversation?"

"Yeah. Since Posar and Nikki have summer homes here, there's a chance that Les might, too." I handed him a yellow tablet and pencil, and—seeing that his bottle was only one quarter full—said, "Will you need any more, uh . . . ?"

"No, I'm fine."

As he began sifting through his mental database of faceless names that fit my description, his writing hand began moving jerkily, like an automaton. After a furious spurt of writing, he stopped suddenly. "How far back in time should I go?"

"Let's start out with no more than five years."

Mr. Memory nodded, putting a big X over the list, starting again. As I slipped out of the room, men in aluminum suits, carrying fire extinguishers, scurried onto the screen. Out in the main room of the basement, the intercom buzzed and Al Emmons's secretary announced that there was a call upstairs for me.

"Hi, Harry," said the voice on the phone in Emmons's office. "Buzz Kerns here. I've got great news. That handwriting sample you gave me could be our break. The graphologist—that is the correct term, isn't it? Graphologist?"

I felt like saying, *"No, fraud is the correct term,"* but instead said, "Yeah, that's right."

"My graphologist consulted an astrologer in Connecticut, and both are developing a profile of the kidnapper. So far they've concluded that the subject is left-handed and was born under the sign of Aries."

It would have been entertaining to hear their reasoning (I was right-handed and born in July), but I let Kerns continue. ". . . and the two of them will soon turn over their data to a numerologist who has access to a mainframe computer . . ."

Great, I thought. A numerologist with a computer makes as

much sense as an alchemist playing with a nuclear reactor. But as long as it kept Kerns busy . . .

"I have more good news," he said. "They've set bail for Cate." He told me the amount.

"That's the best you can do?"

"Hey, we're lucky they set any at all. Can you handle that amount? Cate's husband already said he won't put up any money."

"Yeah, we'll manage. Somehow." Talk about blind optimism, I thought. Especially from a guy who skipped out on a ten-dollar dinner.

But even as I hung up, I knew how I'd finance it. Though I was sure a beseeching call to her husband would change his mind, I knew Cate would hate me for it. Instead, I phoned Al Emmons at home and told him I was finally accepting his offer to buy the illusions from my old touring show. He was ecstatic and said that he'd deliver a check as soon as possible. I called the storage company in California to begin arrangements.

Roberta, Emmons's secretary, was sitting at her desk eating a ham salad sandwich and sipping iced tea from a Thermos. A slender woman in her fifties, she'd been secretary at the Mystic Isle since it opened. I remembered her meekly asking for my autograph the day I arrived for my first engagement here. Her eyes now avoided mine as I hung up.

"Roberta, there's no reason I should keep all those illusions squirreled away. I'm so far behind in storage payments, I'm lucky they didn't auction them off. Instead of gathering dust, they might as well put some money in my pocket. For the last two years, my whole act could fit into a small suitcase."

Roberta nodded politely, then looked away again.

I said, "The illusions will have a good home, don't you think? At least they'll see some life now and then."

The leaden silence in the room was broken by Mr. Memory stumbling through the door. "Ah, there you are," he said, pressing the wall to steady himself. As he spoke, an inordinate amount of time passed between his consonants and vowels. Apparently the magic liquid in his bottle had gone way beyond stimulating his memory.

He showed me his tablet proudly. His writing reminded me of a three-year-old having fun with crayons. I walked to the window, but the added light didn't make his scrawlings any more legible. I considered sending them off to Kerns's graphologist.

"Uh, exactly how many names are here, Mr. Memory?"

"Seven."

I winked at Roberta and said to her, "Any chance you could transcribe this?"

She looked at the sheet and puckered her lips in a silent whistle. "It's a mite hard to read, Mr. Memory," she said. "Do you remember what you wrote?"

He looked deeply insulted.

I said, "Roberta, could you do me one more favor?" She nodded. "I'd like for you to try to get a phone number for each name and then place some short calls to them."

"What should I say?"

"Just leave my name and invite each person to play a game of two-handed poker—*cutthroat* style. I'll be interested in their reactions."

Standing at military attention, Mr. Memory crisply recited his list of names. Roberta's pencil raced across her steno pad, but she wasn't looking at it. She was staring at me with wonder. I decided to answer the question I saw in her eyes. "No, I wasn't joking. I really am selling my illusions."

I headed back downstairs to watch the rest of Mr. Memory's car-crash tape. I needed cheering up.

CHAPTER EIGHTEEN

After the librarian threaded the microfilm machine for me, she left me alone. As I turned the crank, the pages of the *New York Times* whizzed past on the cracked screen. The headlines blurred, blending into basic categories. The verbs seemed to remain the same from day to day, with only the nouns changing. Disaster, pain, scandal, crime, death—the passing pages became the print version of Mr. Memory's car-crash tape.

One story about a magician caught my eye, and my cranking slowed and nearly stopped. Only sheer discipline kept me advancing the film until I reached my destination—an eleven-year-old article about a congressional hearing on fraud.

The testimony centered on Renaissance, Inc., a company that set startling growth records. What brought the company to the committee's attention wasn't the soap products that Renaissance marketed. In fact, the merchandise was priced reasonably and performed well.

It was the company's recruiting methods and profit structure that raised eyebrows. The sales force consisted entirely of part-time salespeople. Renaissance, Inc., was modeled after the multi-level, high-initiation-fee businesses started by a man named Nathan Hardan, who had amassed several fortunes before the turn of the century.

New members of Renaissance were recruited at "parties" held in members' homes. Wild promises of fast money were the theme of these meetings. Disgruntled salespeople testified to the congressional committee about being socked for thousands of dollars in initiation fees, while only a select few ever earned the enormous profits promised.

A business professor told the committee that Renaissance,

Inc.'s high-pressure techniques combined cultism, a chain letter, and the movie *Invasion of the Body Snatchers*. The head of a white-collar bunco squad for the L.A. Police Department testified that the company was essentially the old pyramid scheme, dressed up and taken to Sunday school.

The committee was critical of Renaissance's five-thousand-dollar initiation fee and its lopsided incentive program. Sponsors of new recruits received a sizable commission from the initiation fees, as well as smaller bonuses for new salesmen hired farther down the chain. It was far more profitable to recruit new salespeople than to sell the company's products.

I calculated that for even a fraction of the salesmen to make the outlandish sums promised, every adult and child in the country would have to sign up twice with the company during the next ten years.

I reeled the microfilm a few days ahead to the closing of the hearings. The committee censured Renaissance for its misleading tactics, but recommended no legal action because the promises of wealth were never guaranteed and because a significant volume of products actually were manufactured and sold, as opposed to some pyramid-type frauds which exist solely on paper. One congressman felt that the bad press alone would surely put Renaissance out of business.

I smiled at his naiveté. I had been down that road many times. I knew that businesses like Renaissance will stop thriving when magazines stop running ads with miracle cures for baldness, obesity, and impotence, and talk shows stop booking guests who claim to communicate with dead people and spacemen.

I looked at the copy of today's *Times* on my lap. At the end of the business section was a half-page ad for Renaissance. The company no longer made brash claims of easy wealth. With a photo of a handsome couple in their well-appointed living room, studying a computer printout of profits, the ad invited the reader to dial an 800 number to learn why Renaissance was a wise investment opportunity. It had the stuffy air of an ad for an old brokerage firm. Like an over-the-counter drug that had started out as a snake oil remedy but had stood the test of time, Renaissance had earned respectability simply by being a survivor.

I looked back at the microfilm screen and studied the picture of a man shielding his face with his hat like a criminal. The caption identified him as Lester Zehme, the reclusive founder of

Renaissance. His lawyers and public relations men had done most of his testifying at the hearings.

I looked at the names on the list Roberta had transcribed for Mr. Memory. One of them was Lester Zehme. Zehme was the only one not puzzled by Roberta's cryptic phone call inviting him to play poker with a man named Harry. Zehme had laughed, said, "Send him over," and hung up.

The final paragraphs of the article gave background on Nathan Hardan, the turn-of-the century huckster whose pyramid businesses Zehme had modeled Renaissance after. In his later years, Hardan went off the deep end, claiming he'd been contacted by beings from another galaxy. He sold shares in a company that guaranteed passage to Mars to escape the holocaust of an imminent alien invasion. Incredibly, Hardan even turned a profit from this, his final and wildest scheme. To some people, the disappearance of several investors, including Hardan's wife, only added credence to his claims of interplanetary travel. There wasn't enough evidence for an indictment.

Rewinding the film, I stopped at a picture of a magician sitting in a coffin in a shopping mall in Massachusetts. The coffin would be sealed and buried for ten days in the mall's tropical garden. As a "going-away" gift for his beautiful assistant, the magician materialized a gold ring with a ruby surrounded by twenty-four diamonds.

I wondered if Cate still had that ring.

I signaled for the librarian and asked her to show me how to make copies from the microfilm. I wanted a copy of the Renaissance articles. And one of the picture of that young magician in the coffin.

I decided to make one stop before visiting Zehme's summer home. But as I turned onto O'Malley Street, I hit a detour. I parked up the block and walked back to the intersection where a bored policeman stood in front of a wooden barricade, tooting his whistle to reroute traffic away from the fire trucks and police cars a half block behind him. Black smoke cloaked an office building in the distance.

"What building's that?" I asked.

The cop let his whistle drop from his teeth, but continued directing traffic. "The Wallace Trust Building. If you have an appointment there, you're too late, buddy."

"Anyone hurt?"

"Nah, just some minor smoke inhalation. The building's not a total loss. Just a few offices gutted."

"Any idea of the cause?"

He shook his head. "It's too early to tell. They only know that it was started on the fourth floor."

"*Was* started? They suspect arson?"

The cop smiled patronizingly. "Nowadays, *every* fire investigation starts out with the suspicion of arson."

"I'm new around here. Would 2415 happen to be the street number of the Wallace Building?"

"Yeah. That's it. You sure you're not headed there?"

"Not anymore," I said, and started back toward my van. Anything of interest to me in the Wallace Trust Building would now be ash and cinders. Lisa South's office was on the fourth floor. Used to be, that is.

From a pay phone in a restaurant a half mile from Zehme's house, I dialed his number and let it ring a dozen times before hanging up. I returned to my van and continued to his place. Zehme lived in an area not so exclusive as Lisa South's. Despite the fortune he had amassed by sitting for years at the top of the Renaissance pyramid, his house was plain and unobtrusive. The boxy gray structure, with its many tiny, dark windows, was nearly hidden from the roadside by high shrubbery. There was no house number on the stone pillars flanking his driveway, no big Z on the gate to reassure me I was at the right place. I parked around the corner, well off the road, and hoped my rusting van wouldn't be towed away as an abandoned vehicle.

I passed through the gate and circled around the opaque wall of shrubs to the rear of the house. I knocked long and loud at the back door. No one answered. Not seeing any alarm system, I reached for my lock picks. The lock surprised me, putting up more resistance than the front door of a jewelry store. After ten minutes which seemed like two hours I heard the satisfying click of the latch pulling away from the doorjamb.

Hearing nothing other than the twitter of birds on the lawn, I glided the door open a few inches and squeezed through. I closed it behind me, not quite engaging the latch. I was on a small landing. Steps to my right led to the basement. Those on my left headed up a few feet to a door—probably the kitchen. Taking care not to creak boards, I took several seconds to climb the five steps. I twisted the doorknob as though it was a windup key of a fragile old music box. I pulled the door open, but couldn't see any of the kitchen. That's because Zehme's maid—all two hundred fifty pounds of her—was blocking my view.

She didn't ask my name, nor my business. With her hands on her ample hips, she stared at me—*through me*, to be precise. Ignoring my story about being a gas meter reader who had forgotten his clipboard, she gave me a vacant nod and walked away. Figuring it was the polite thing to do, I followed.

Zehme's house was more spacious than it appeared from the outside. Following the maid down a carpeted hallway, I passed eight rooms and then crossed a sitting room with silk-covered chairs and shelves of blue Oriental figurines. We ended up in what I thought was an office, judging by the calendar on the wall, the file cabinet, and the three shelves full of books. Still silent, the maid left me alone, closing the door.

A small writing table stood under a window with an antique telephone, a stack of stationery, an appointment book, and a small sign that said "Thank you for not smoking." On the wall near the table was a picture in a brass frame. I thought it was a miniature oil painting, but closer examination revealed that it was a photograph whose color had been enhanced by eccentric lighting. The man in the photo was Les, the poker player. The woman beside him was a brunette with hair swept severely up to the side. She wore a strapless chiffon dress that was stylishly revealing. She was young enough to be his daughter—his granddaughter, even. Her arms were entwined possessively around his waist and she gazed longingly into his eyes. Granddaughter, she wasn't.

Dominating the opposite wall was a painting of a man in shirt-sleeves and a bow tie, sitting at an ancient manual typewriter. The brass nameplate below the painting said, "Nathan Hardan"—Zehme's role model. The other paintings in the room were a hodgepodge of traditional and contemporary styles.

Listening for approaching footsteps, I flipped open Zehme's appointment book to the day of the poker game. Only one word was entered for that date: *Lesson.* No mention of playing poker. *Lesson* appeared several times in preceding weeks, as well as the word *golf.* I assumed that Zehme was spending a fortune in lessons to straighten out the hook in his drive.

On a wall shelf to the right were ten glass cases, each containing a single bar of Renaissance Soap. I turned the last case around and saw that on the back of the soap wrapper was a coupon offering a children's magic kit in exchange for one hundred soap wrappers. It was a recent coupon. I wondered if I had in some small way inspired Zehme to run the offer.

In a corner closet, I found a metal shelf full of typing paper, typewriter ribbons, envelopes, and other office supplies. In the back of the closet sat two plastic cases with handles. One contained a portable laptop computer with a flip-up LCD screen. The other contained a letter-quality printer. I checked the daisy wheel on the printer. It was a normal typewriter style—nothing like the printing in the ransom note.

Hearing steps in the hallway, I shut the closet door and walked quickly to the middle of the room. Lester Zehme, wearing a red golf shirt and a pair of crazy-quilt checkered pants, strode into the office. His quick handshake sent a twinge of pain through my knuckles. He gestured at two swivel chairs in front of the writing desk. As I sat down, he took a clipboard from one of the bookcases, studied it for a moment, and shoved it back on the shelf.

"My name's Harry—"

He cut me off, like a tennis player slamming back an easy lob. "I know who you are. My question, is what took you so long? I've got better things to do than wait for you to slink through my yard and pick my back door lock. If you think that lock was tough, you should have tried my front door."

Wonderful, I thought. A few hecklers like him at every show and I wouldn't last another year in magic. Zehme flipped open his file cabinet, withdrew a folder, and dropped it on my lap. My name was typed on the label. The folder contained photocopies of news articles about me, mostly covering publicity stunts to promote my touring show several years ago. The copies were clear and highly defined, unlike the smudged ones I'd made from the microfilm today.

Zehme picked up one of the articles and stared at it. It featured a photo of Cate, dressed in a leggy parody of the magician's tuxedo. She wore a bow tie clinched around her neck and a ruffled shirt that revealed a lot of cleavage. I didn't like the smirk on Zehme's face as his thumbs made slow circles along the edges of the picture.

"When I read in the paper about the murder of poor Lisa South, I figured you were the magician—Harry Colderwood—they were referring to. Too big a coincidence for a stranger named Harry to show up at our poker game and clean us all out." He pointed to the dossier on my lap. "I asked a college intern with my company to do some research on you."

"Your company is Renaissance, Inc.?"

"I see you've done your homework, too."

"Some of it. But I still don't know why a busy man like you is wasting his time running a check on a nightclub magician . . . or why you're playing in poker games for stakes that couldn't be more than pocket change for you."

He glanced out the window at a man stooped over the flower garden in the yard. "I'm not the total workaholic I used to be. When a company like Renaissance reaches a certain level of success, a lot of young upstarts begin chipping away at your authority. The last few years I've grown weary trying to maintain total control of my power base. I've intentionally let some of it erode. In effect, I'm retiring a little at a time. Age changes your attitude. So does a heart that occasionally acts like an engine missing two cylinders." He smiled at the picture of the couple on the wall. "But what really made me slow down and enjoy life was falling in love and getting married for what I know will be the last time. Before meeting Ali, I was working too hard to do much traveling or fishing or golfing. She is teaching me to appreciate life . . . to learn new things just for the sheer pleasure of it."

Pointing to the bookshelf behind him, he said, "Ali has a wide variety of interests. She's got me reading and thinking about stuff I'd never have dreamed of a few years ago."

I looked at the bookcase. Most of the books were paperbacks with gaudy covers. Their themes ran the gamut of paranormal subjects from astrology to faith healing to reincarnation. "Nothing to be embarrassed about," I said. "I once had a secret collection of girlie magazines. I never forgave my mom for trashing them. But I'd have grown out of them in a few years, as I'm sure you will with this drivel."

"Nonsense," he said, offended. "Surely a man of your profession realizes there's more to this wonderful world than what your five senses tell you."

"You've got it backwards, Zehme. A man of my profession

knows how easily those five senses can trick the mind. You're right, the world *is* wonderful. Trouble is, some people are too lazy to figure out how it really works, so they gum it up with false worlds of their own creation.''

Zehme smiled patiently. ''Perhaps when you near the end of your journey through this cruel life, you'll find comfort in books like those.''

''The only comfort they'll ever provide me is to prop open a window on a hot day.''

He scooted his chair closer and leaned forward, his eyes ablaze with an intensity that belied his earlier talk of retirement. ''How much do you really know about my company?''

''I've read articles that—''

''Bah! So-called journalism. Prejudiced blather from outsiders who'd starve if their measly salaries ever stopped trickling in. Let me tell you the *real* story behind Renaissance. . . .'' He sat up straighter, his speech growing forceful, his gestures more vigorous. He told me that when he started his company, he used a rented trailer for a warehouse. Neglecting to mention the fraud allegations, he talked proudly of the tremendous growth of Renaissance and of how many ''partners''—the company term for salespeople—had become millionaires. His prediction of the company's future was glowing: soaring profits, product expansion, and more facilities to train the sales force. Taking a pen and notepad from his pocket, he said, ''What night is most convenient for you?''

''For what?''

''To attend a meeting about how my company can enrich your life.'' He read a list of addresses where introductory meetings were being held in coming weeks—all in people's homes.

''Sorry, I pass.''

Zehme shrugged and dropped the notepad back in his pocket. ''For the past thirty years, I always make it a point to invite everyone I meet to hear the Renaissance story . . . regardless of whether I'm standing at a bus stop, in an elevator, or in a reception line at the governor's inaugural ball. I leave no stone unturned. You'd be surprised how many people write me letters years later, thanking me for the marvelous opportunity.''

''What about the poker game? Were you the one who sent the invitations to that 'marvelous opportunity'?''

His face darkened. ''Ah, yes,'' he said, ''the game. That, I'm afraid, is a different matter. You see, as founder of Renaissance, it's tiring being a constant champion of the free-enterprise system. The poker game, although short-lived, was a marvelous way to relax. It was one place where I could lose without fear of tarnishing my image.''

''Any chance that Lisa South tried to tarnish that image?''

He studied my face as though it were an outrageous bill he was debating whether to pay. ''I'm afraid I don't get you.''

As I told him about the open bathroom window at the poker game, the door edged open and a tabby cat crept into the room. Zehme patted his lap and the cat hopped up and settled down for a nap. Both the cat's eyes and Zehme's looked glassy and distant as he stroked it beneath its chin.

''Did you know Lisa South?'' I asked.

''Yes, somewhat. We were on speaking terms. In a small town like this, it was inevitable we'd become acquainted.''

''So you were just two people who'd nod politely while passing in the supermarket, right?''

''Something like that. You might say we met at a bus stop.''

''You're kidding. You actually invited Lisa South to be a Renaissance salesman?''

''As I said, I ask *everybody*. Renaissance isn't a get-rich-quick scheme that caters to down-and-outs with nowhere to turn. Our most successful sales reps are people who already run profitable businesses. Some are even doctors and lawyers.''

The maid tromped in, carrying a silver tray loaded with bottles, balls of cotton, and a package of syringes. She stood stiffly beside his chair as Zehme talked soothingly to the cat. He wet a cotton ball with a bottle of alcohol from the tray and wiped it on the rubber seal of a vial labeled *Insulin*. Plunging a syringe into the vial he drew out a few units of insulin. He pinched the fur above the cat's rear leg and expertly slid the needle in, depressing the plunger. The cat yawned, not even twitching at the shot. Zehme dropped the hypodermic on the tray, and the maid left hastily.

Zehme said, ''His name's Izzy, named after the cat in those TV commercials.'' He gestured at a catfood calendar hanging on the wall. ''Unfortunately, Izzy is a diabetic. He wouldn't last long without his daily injection. As much as my maid and Ali love him, they don't have the stomach to give him his shot.'' He scratched the cat behind the ears, and it reared its head to meet his fingers. "You asked me about Lisa South. A nasty thing, her murder. The papers say your former assistant, Cate, is taking the rap for it. I wish you luck in clearing her name. I wish I could be of more help."

When I nodded thanks, he said, "If the organizer of the poker game is the killer, there won't be any more games, will there? You and I will probably never see each other again."

"Oh, maybe you'll catch my act at the Mystic Isle."

He smiled. "That's doubtful. Ali and I keep to ourselves. We rarely go out. After years of twenty-hour workdays, I'm only starting to appreciate the meaning of the word 'peace.' You see, Ali is my third wife, and I have every intention of her being the last. I hate sharing her with anyone. The thought of dying alone scares the hell out of me."

Zehme rubbed the cat under its chin, but Izzy had apparently reached his own peace quota for the day. The cat spat at him and shrank from his touch. Zehme tried to pet the cat again, and Izzy gave him a roundhouse swipe with its paw, leaving little bloody lines across the back of his hand. With a roar, Zehme lunged for the cat's neck, but it was like trying to catch smoke. Izzy sprang off his lap, stabbing Zehme's thighs with its back claws. Zehme jumped up and took a wild kick at the cat and missed, jamming his toes into the reading table and scattering papers and pencils. An old hand at this game, Izzy trotted boldly across the floor and stopped at the door. The cat jabbed its nose into the opening, nudged the door open, and cruised out of the room like an employee leaving the office after a hard day's work.

Taking his seat again, Zehme muttered that he was going to fix Izzy good someday. Then, as if trying to prove that he wasn't really such a bad guy, he spent the next fifteen minutes advising me on investment strategies—smart ways to spend all the big entertainment bucks he thought I was earning. Growing bored with plans for money I didn't have, I looked out the window. The day was heating up under a cloudless sky. I watched the gardener lovingly examine his flowers, briefly holding each stem between his fingers like the stem of a wineglass.

The maid stuck her head in and announced dinner. Zehme invited me to stay, but I begged off. As we walked down the hall, he said he had no idea who had organized the poker game, but if he learned anything new, he'd be in touch. He tried one more time to persuade me to attend a Renaissance meeting.

I left the same way I came in, locking the back door behind me. Outside, the gardener was now trimming the grass around a rosebush with a pair of household scissors. To his right stood a camera on a tripod.

"Do you keep a photographic record of your flowers?" I asked.

A slight man in a crinkled fishing hat, the gardener grunted and continued snipping. "Not me," he said. "That camera is one of Mrs. Z's hobbies." He pointed to the other side of the lawn where a lithe brunette lay prone on a blanket, her eyes closed. I could almost see the heat shimmer off her bronzed body. Her bikini top was untied in back. Staring at her sleek figure, I noticed a few places that could use more suntan oil. A bottle of lotion lay beside her, but I decided not to volunteer my services.

I touched the top of the camera, and it was hot from the sun. "Mrs. Zehme has a short attention span?" I asked.

The gardener looked me over, trying to decide whether I was a friend of Zehme's. He quickly saw that it was okay to talk. "Considering the number of hobbies Mrs. Z has, it's a wonder she has time for anything. On a hot day like this, she loses interest in whatever she's doing in about ten minutes. Then she usually suns herself or goes to her air-conditioned exercise room to hop around to one of those aerobics tapes. She sleeps a lot, too. Particularly after one of her—her sick spells."

"What hobbies does she have?"

"All sorts. Besides taking pictures of flowers, there's pottery and oil painting. A year ago a guy used to come and give her piano lessons twice a week. Lately she's taken up sewing. She makes a lot of fancy dresses . . . which doesn't make sense because Mr. Z won't take her anywhere." He brushed away grass clippings from the scissor blades and stood up. "He treats that woman like one of the flowers in this garden. It's like he planted her here at this estate and is getting a kick out of watching her dry up and wither away."

I looked past Ali Zehme to the farthest corner of the yard, at a somber white-and-brown gazebo. I said, "That gazebo looks run-down compared to the rest of this place. You'd think Mrs. Zehme would adopt it as one of her hobbies and fix it up a little. A fresh coat of paint, at least."

"Gazebo? Oh, you mean *that?* No, Mrs. Z won't go near that.
It's not really a gazebo."

"Oh?"

"It's a cemetery."

As I walked away, the gardener started snipping faster, sounding like a barber on a profitable Saturday morning.

Ali Zehme didn't stir as I moved softly past and approached the round wooden structure I'd mistaken for a gazebo. A tiny wooden cross was planted in the grass beside the entrance. Inside, the air was cool, like a cave. More crosses, and slabs of engraved stone—the size of books—jutted from the bare, hard ground. The burial plots were too small and closely grouped for humans. The oldest stone dated back eight years. Each bore the same name—Izzy, and the stones went all the way up to Izzy the Sixth.

Izzy the Cat had only seven lives, not nine . . . at least in the Zehme household.

CHAPTER NINETEEN

Applause from the main room of the Mystic Isle filtered up through the floor into Al Emmons's office. I sat with my feet on his desk, shoes off. The desk was covered with black velvet, just like the pads used by close-up magicians to make their props more visible and easier to handle. Emmons was a closet magician. Few visitors left his office without being subjected to his tedious pea-and-shell routine. Fortunately, Emmons was a better businessman than magician or the club would have gone bust in a week.

When it came to booking talent—and buying stage equipment—Emmon could always smell a great deal. He'd acted fast after I accepted his offer. On her way home from the office, Roberta had dropped off at my hotel a certified check for the full amount—which I'd quickly disposed of. I looked down at the legal papers officially transferring my old illusion show to Emmon. Only a few dotted lines awaited my signature.

Emmons was downstairs now, playing the congenial host to club patrons. His office door had been locked when I arrived, but it was a piece of cake. An eighth-grader with a thin comb could have popped the lock. Emmons never bothered with elaborate security devices—not in a club full of magicians.

I made a feeble attempt to decipher the legal wording of the sales agreement, but gave up, figuring that sentences with more than four semicolons weren't worth reading, anyway. I took the biggest pen on Emmons's desk and scrawled my name on each copy of the contract.

When I finished, I shut my eyes and sat back, letting the memories of my old illusions wash over me: the Jamison Levitation—with smooth-running gears and a motor that never "talked," and

113

the Crystal Tomb—a Plexiglas coffin built by a casket manufacturer who was also a magician. Cate used to magically appear in it with a flash of blue fire.

I ticked off the illusions one by one in my head. Each had involved Cate in some way. After we split, I'd never used them again. It now seemed fitting to help her by selling them.

The desk phone rang, sounding like an electronic bird in pain. I sunk deeper in the chair, unwilling to emerge from my nostalgic wallowing. Finally I picked up the receiver and said hello.

"Is this the Mystic Isle?" a woman said. Her voice was sluggish, but not from liquor. Instead of one drink too many, I thought she had swallowed one pill too many.

"Yes."

"I'd like to speak to one of your performers. His name is Harry Colderwood."

Always trying to stay a jump ahead of my creditors, I said, "Who's calling, please?"

"My name is Ali Zehme."

My feet dropped off the desk and I sat up. In two seconds I had a pen in my hand and a cigarette in my mouth. "Mrs. Zehme, this is Harry speaking."

"Call me Ali, please. Tell me, do you always act as your own secretary?"

"When you owe as much money as me, you need all the buffers you can get."

"I know what you mean."

"About what? Owing money or having buffers?"

"A little of both. The years before I met Lester were rather lean."

Over the phone, I heard a hammer pounding and a power saw chewing through wood. "Where are you calling from?"

"Home. From a basement phone. Lester is having the basement redone. It's the third time in five years. That man never seems satisfied with the way things are."

If she had called to unload her woes of married life, I'd gladly lend a sympathetic ear, providing she answered some questions about her husband, I slipped on my shoes without tying them and tapped my cigarette on the desktop. I snapped my fingers in front of a miniature magician holding a wand—Emmons's cigarette lighter. An audio sensor tripped a relay and a flame popped out of the wand. I leaned over, lit up, and snapped my fingers again. The flame vanished. I wished all magic could be so easy.

Ali raised her voice to compete with a fresh blast from the saw. "I wasn't kidding when I said things were lean before I met Lester. I grew up in a neighborhood that's since been gutted by arsonists and never rebuilt. I was fortunate that, before graduation, a high school counselor got me involved in a secretarial training program. As soon as I could, I moved away from there and got a job with a travel agency in New York where I shared an apartment with three other girls. All of us had jobs with good working conditions but poor wages. My roommates constantly complained about the apartment, the neighborhood, and their jobs, but it all seemed quite nice to me. Compared to some of the kids I grew up with, I had made it. Some were heavily into dope. Some were selling themselves—and whatever else they could—on the street. Many of my childhood friends joined gangs. Some plain never made it past the age of eighteen. During those years, the kind of life I have today seemed as remote a possibility as marrying into royalty."

"How'd you meet Lester Zehme?"

"It was six years ago. At a Renaissance meeting. One of my roomies was dating a sales rep for the company, and she conned me into going. The meeting was at her boyfriend's apartment, and I went just to appease her. It was a big bore. Everyone was shocked when Lester Zehme himself—founder of the whole damn company—showed up. It's one of his practices to walk in unannounced at company functions, even lowly sales meetings. Everybody treated him like a god that night . . . except me. I was tired and wanted to go home and hit the sack. Because I ignored him, I must have been an irresistible challenge to Lester. He introduced himself to me during cocktails after the meeting. He refused to listen to my complaints about being tired, and we talked for an hour and a half. I was pleasantly surprised to find myself in the most fascinating conversation of my life. Lester has such a talent for making people feel good about themselves. He was so charming, I easily saw how he could spearhead a company whose primary goal is persuading people to accept the illogical. He called me five times that week, until I finally accepted a date. Three weeks later he proposed."

"And you accepted?"

"Of course. Do you think I'd ruin a storybook ending to my

own biography? Lester still refers to the night we met as the most profitable sales meeting in company history.''

I let Ali Zehme relive her memories for a few moments as I listened to the remodelers drive in nails. Then I said, ''How did you know to call me?''

''You thought I was asleep on that blanket, but I wasn't. I later asked Lester who the stranger was tramping through our yard. He told me your name and that he was hiring you to perform magic for a company promotion. Poor Lester thinks that all I do all day is soak up the sun and take pictures of flowers. He doesn't give me credit for even reading the newspaper. I recognized your name right away as being mixed up in that local murder.''

''That's why you called? Because of Lisa South?''

''Yes.'' She lowered her voice until it barely competed with the power tools. ''I've got to know if Lester is involved in that case.''

I stubbed out my butt in the top hat at the base of the magician lighter. ''I'm sorry, Ali. I'm afraid he is.''

''Perhaps it would help if I answered some questions.''

''I'm sure it would. But let me warn you, the questions won't be delicate.''

She chuckled. ''A delicate person I'm not, Harry . . . regardless of what Lester may say. You really must tell me what you know about him.''

''If you want to swap information, it's okay by me.''

''Deal.'' For a long time there was silence. Then she said softly, ''You first.''

''Mrs. . . . I mean, Ali, are you sure about this? He's your husband and maybe—''

''Harry, I've grown to love Lester over the years. And he loves me. But his way of showing love is often incompatible with mine. He treats me like a queen and tries to shield me from the pain and ugliness in life. He considers it his personal mission to make up for my hard years. Of course, his devotion is flattering, but sometimes the truth gets lost in his efforts. He shields me from parts of himself he's ashamed of. Sometimes I'm not sure who I married. I really must know how deeply he's involved in that killing.''

''Fair enough.'' I told her about the poker game and how it was connected with the murder, leaving out the identities of the other players. In return she told me what she knew of Zehme's whereabouts during the past weeks. She said that on the dates of the poker games, Zehme had been gone during the day as well as at night. I asked her about the word *lesson* on his calendar.

"You really have been probing, haven't you? I peeked at his date book too, and checked with the golf pro at Lester's club. He says Lester plays regularly but isn't taking lessons."

"Did Lester say what he was doing those evenings?"

"He told me he was dropping in on sales meetings. I had no reason to doubt him, considering all the surprise visits he makes."

"Did you know he was acquainted with Lisa South?"

Ali sighed. "I'm afraid they were more than acquainted. A few weeks ago, Lester seemed depressed. I asked if he was sick, and he blamed it on indigestion. But that's not like him. He's never had a sick day since I met him. He went out that night, and, on impulse, I had him followed."

"You hired a detective?"

"No. I got the maid to drive me. We have two cars, but neither Lester nor I know how to drive."

"Does he have a chauffeur?"

"Technically, no. Lester uses anyone on the house staff who's available at the time. The gardener was driving Lester the night I followed him."

I described the limo that took me to the poker game and asked if they owned a car like that.

"No. We have a Mercedes and a Lincoln."

"Where did Lester go that night?"

"Directly to Lisa South's house. He stayed for two hours."

"Did you ever confront him about it?"

"No. I felt too damn guilty about following him. I'd never done anything like that before. But upon hearing of Lisa South's murder, I decided to find out the truth . . . no matter what. Perhaps Lester was having an affair with her, just as Cate Fleming's husband had been. But, according to the newspapers, Fleming has an alibi. My husband doesn't. All Lester has is this phantom poker game. If you learn anything about him—even bad news—please let me know. He'd never confide in me. He's so afraid I'll see him in a bad light . . . afraid I'll leave him. I need to *know*, Harry. I just need to know." Her voice quavered, and her rambling words became lost in sobs, which she tried to control by taking deep breaths. She managed to say, "I love him so much,'' and then she clicked off. In my mind I saw her shuffling to the bathroom for another glass of water . . . and another visit to the medicine cabinet.

As though on cue, the audience downstairs erupted into applause. *But what are they applauding?* I thought. The devotion of a loving wife? Or the convincing performance of an actress concealing coldness with crocodile tears? The next time I talked to her, I intended to find out how much and what kind of drugs she was using.

I closed my eyes and listened to the waltz music, letting mental images of Edward and his parasols soothe the internal jangling caused by Ali's call—a call that added Ali herself to the suspect list. Her motive—jealousy.

I was snuffing out another cigarette in the magician's top hat when the office door opened. A woman's voice said, ''Harry, what are you doing here? Thinking of moving into management?''

I jerked back in my seat and knocked over the little magician, spilling all the ashes. Cate was standing in the doorway, looking pale and exhausted. Something was different about her, but I wasn't sure what. Then I realized she was wearing all the jewelry that the police had confiscated: a flat wide bracelet, a silver necklace, and a pair of turquoise earrings. No ruby ring with diamonds, though.

She moved to the desk and placed both palms flat on top, ignoring the ashes. ''Thanks for bailing me out. How'd you manage it? Didn't sell all your tricks, did you?'' She said this with a laugh.

''As a matter of fact, I did,'' I said quietly.

She looked for the curl of my lip or the arching of my brow that would say I was joking. But my only reaction was a steady, sober stare. Her face fell, and she covered her eyes with her hand. I rushed around the desk to her. As we hugged, she smudged ashes over the back of my tuxedo shirt. Her body trembled and she couldn't control her sniffling.

''Cate, I promised I'd find who did this to you. Just like magic. Now don't worry. Those junky old illusions aren't the kind of magic we need to solve this, anyway.''

The closing notes of Edward's music brought cheers and whistles. There was a knock at the door and Al Emmons's voice said, ''Why the hell's this locked? Harry, are you in there? Someone said you were up here. Harry, do you hear me? You've got to go on next. Mr. Memory's got a snootful. He can't even remember his own name, let alone those of the people in the audience.''

"The show must go on," I whispered in Cate's ear.

"Trouble is, Harry," she said with a tired smile, "the show's never over for you."

CHAPTER TWENTY

Cate trailed behind as I ran down the steps two at a time, heading for the main floor at the rear of the Mystic Isle. The P.A. system was now pumping out mood music that was better suited for Saturday morning at the supermarket. The audience was puzzled by the lag in the show. As the music faded, I heard the bump of a microphone being hastily detached from its stand, followed by the basso profundo voice of the Incredible Zinderneuf, resident MC of the Mystic Isle. Zinderneuf stumbled over his first words, but within seconds he regained his composure and was shooting out one-liners with the force and regularity of a baseball pitching machine. By the time Cate and I reached the bottom of the steps, the audience was applauding Zinderneuf as he performed a disappearing routine with a giant silver dollar.

We entered a narrow, dark hallway that extended the whole way to the backstage area. It was packed with waiters, entertainers, and customers looking for the rest rooms. As I stooped to tie my shoelaces, Zinderneuf was beginning a cut-and-restored ribbon trick I knew he hadn't done in five years. I pointed at a door with an Exit sign above it and said, "We'll make better time this way, Cate."

Outside, we eased along the walkway between the club and the adjacent office building, careful not to wrench our ankles on the loose bricks that had fallen from both buildings. Water drops pelted my head and shoulders. Cate squeezed my hand and I slowed down. Reaching the stage door, I checked my pockets and the loads hidden under my coat, making sure all my props were in place. To make up for Mr. Memory's absence, Al Emmons would expect everyone to play longer. That meant I'd have to dig something else from my trunk of spare equipment down in my dressing room.

I opened the stage door and was greeted by the boozy, smoky air of my workplace. I looked back at Cate. The brisk run had restored some color to her cheeks and her eyes were bright. I was struck with the sudden urge to just keep running, to never come back to this town.

I felt a pulsing in her hand that seemed to match my heartbeat. Without going inside, I let the door hiss shut, shutting off Zinderneuf's bantering, leaving us alone in the dripping, dark walkway. I said "Why don't we just forget this place? I don't need it. I'm just one of a dozen interchangeable acts. The audience doesn't care. They don't even remember our names. Let's just have dinner and—"

Cate shook her head. "What are you talking about? You've already gotten yourself blackballed off TV. What's left if the club circuit loses faith in you?"

I grinned. "Kid shows. Haven't you heard? There's tons and tons of money in Cub Scout banquets."

Opening the door, I reentered the musty, acrid air of show biz. I breathed deeply and felt a new energy; then I coughed.

Al Emmons hovered over me as I rooted through my trunk. He said a curt hello to Cate, as if six years hadn't passed, and she was still part of my act. He waved a fresh set of contracts at me. "Harry, my lawyer just gave me these. They have to be signed, too. Boy, another deal like this and I'll have to add a new floor to my warehouse. Hey, Harry, you'd better get a move on. The crowd's getting tired of Zinderneuf's face."

I rummaged through my truck some more and tossed out a box containing a dozen rubber chickens—a gift from a West Coast magician who performed an entire act with them. He wrung laughs from the chickens the way a violinist coaxes music from his instrument.

Finding a foot-long pen in my trunk, I scratched my name in purple on Emmons's contracts. Satisfied, he drifted away.

Cate touched my shoulder. "One thing I have to know. Have you narrowed the list of suspects?"

"No. I'm afraid the list has expanded. It—oh, here they are." I pulled out the box of feather flowers I was looking for. I closed the trunk and went out into the main room of the basement. I stuck my head in the next dressing room and saw Mr. Memory sprawled on the couch. He was softly singing "Hickory-dickory-dock. The mouse ran up the clock. The clock struck one and—" He cleared his throat. "The clock struck one . . . For crissakes, what's next?" He looked up at me and waved merrily. "Harry, I can't remember what's next. Can you imagine? I *can't* remember!"

For the first time since we'd met, Mr. Memory seemed truly happy.

On our way upstairs, I quickly told Cate about the other poker players.

"What about this Zehme?" she asked. "I can see why his wife might have a motive. But what about him?"

"I'm not certain. He's such a genius at turning public criticism to his advantage, I can't imagine Lisa South digging up anything that could hurt him. Maybe his wife's suspicions are correct. Maybe he was having an affair with Lisa, and something came between them. Perhaps she found another man and told him to get lost."

I searched the wings for Ed McClenahan, the stagehand who had taped the rock video for me. A woman I didn't recognize shone a flashlight in my eyes and whispered that McClenahan had called off sick tonight and that she was filling in.

The Incredible Zinderneuf took a deep bow, basking in his final applause. Sweat rained from his chin as he walked offstage and kept his wide grin even when out of sight of the audience. If Emmons had asked, Zinderneuf would have gladly done another twenty minutes. Zinderneuf loved challenges.

"I'm going to need your help," I said to Cate.

She stiffened and backed away. "Absolutely not. Six years ago I said I'd never share the stage with you again, and I meant it. I don't need any reminders of why I made that decision. Even a batboy at the ballpark is treated with more respect than a magician's assistant."

"No, no. I don't need help with my act. I need help with the big trick you and I'll be cooking up soon—the trick of proving your innocence. I've got some ideas."

"Right now, here's the only help I can give you," she said and kissed me gently on the cheek.

A backstage announcer with a ringmaster's voice shouted my name into his microphone, and something electric in my spine caused me to pull away from Cate. I absently touched my cheek where she had kissed it. As I hurried onstage, I felt the usual thrill, as though I were catapulting out of a jet at Mach 3. In the opening minutes of my act, I made several mistakes and blamed them on the mad scurry from Emmons's office. They weren't the kind of errors an audience would notice, but they were enough to throw off my rhythm. They spelled the difference between thunderous applause and boy-I'm-glad-this-act-is-over applause. In my mind, I saw the Dean Brothers downstairs, watching me on the closed-circuit TV, snickering and calling me a has-been. I looked offstage and saw that even Cate's attention was straying from the incessant billiard balls and cards and scarfs that I was pulling out of the air.

I was grateful when I heard the closing bars of my recorded music. Because of my unscheduled trick, I decided against my usual vanish-in-smoke finish. A stagehand brought out a mike and stand, and I adjusted its height. Speaking to the audience for the first time, I requested help from an audience volunteer. I looked past the glare of the footlights and chose the most likely candidate—a shy-looking man with a small mouth and round eyes. As he climbed the steps to the stage, I noticed that he was shorter and older (pushing late sixties, at least) than I at first thought. He wore a plaid shirt with wide red suspenders. When he stumbled on the top step, his embarrassed grin got a belly laugh from the audience. I knew I had chosen well.

He told me his name was Hayden Miller. I patted him on the back and announced that I was going to give him a lesson in sleight of hand. I challenged him to watch closely. He positioned his feet firmly on the stage and hunched forward, as if waiting for the starting gun in a footrace. His eyes dutifully followed my fingers as I reached into the air and plucked a rose from no-where. He stretched out his hand as I started to give it to him. Suddenly the rose was gone . . . at least from his point of view.

I then did the same thing with another flower, and he was just as baffled. I repeated this several more times, with the audience laughing louder each time. This routine was one of the few in magic where everyone knew how the trick was done *except* the volunteer. I accomplished the vanish of the rose by raising it a few inches above his forehead, out of his peripheral vision. Momentarily covering the flower with my other hand, I flicked it over his head. Everybody but the helpless volunteer saw where the flower went.

After milking the trick for all the laughs I could get, I normally requested my helper to turn around. The bewilderment on his face usually brought the house down. Instead of the expected pile of flowers on the floor behind the volunteer, the audience would see that the roses were all dangling from the assistant's back. They were attached by thin cords of elastic I had stuck on with adhesive tape when I patted him on the back at the start of the routine.

But tonight was different. The audience, still restless from the delay in the show, had an unusually cruel bent. I overheard such comments as *"How can anyone be so dumb?"* and *"That dip must be blind."* On his return trip to his seat, Hayden Miller would definitely be in for some heckling.

With each vanishing rose, the audience grew more belligerent and Miller grew more uncomfortable. With his jaw cocked to the side and his eyes glued to my hands, he leaned closer and concentrated, not realizing that this made it even easier for me to perform the trick. The little man reached in his pocket and donned a pair of thick glasses that made his eyes look even beadier. The audience hooted and whooped at him. That's when I called it quits.

I whispered, "It's just a trick, Hayden. Simple when you know how. Look." I reached behind and held up one of the roses dangling from his back. A smile played across his face as it dawned on him how it was done. I pulled a handful of cigars out of the air and stuffed them in his shirt pocket as a souvenir. After gently removing the small garden of roses from his back, I wished him well and asked the audience to clap for him as he returned to his seat. The applause was weak as the audience tried to imagine why the routine had ended so flat. But at least Hayden Miller had enjoyed his brief time in the limelight—and no one heckled him.

After I bowed and made my exit, the stage manager said, "Harry, there's a call for you on the pay phone downstairs."

Cate was leaning against the wall by the stairway, trying not to be tramped on by a baby leopard being loaded into an illusion. "What the hell was that all about?" she said. "That ending really fizzled."

I shrugged my shoulders, not wanting to explain that my unexpected sympathy for Miller may have been a result of my futile attempts to unravel the murder of Lisa South. I was learning firsthand how it feels to be played the patsy . . . to be the only one left out of a big secret.

"You aren't the same magician you were six years ago," Cate said.

Her words stung. But as she pressed her lips against my cheek and slid them across to my mouth, I realized that she had paid me a compliment. I returned the kiss and she said, "You'd better get that call."

Downstairs, I was glad to see that Mr. Memory was feeling better. He was now sitting cross-legged in front of the TV, munching a doughnut and watching a quiz show. He shook his head at the faulty memories of the panelists. With his mouth full, he said, "Thanks for standing in for me. Remind me to repay the favor some day." As if Mr. Memory needed reminding of anything but his manners.

The pay phone in the corner was off the hook, the handset dangling. I picked it up and said, "Hello."

"Harry, this is Ed McClenahan."

"Ed, where the hell've you been? I brought a special guest tonight to meet you. Second thought, maybe you were better off taking the night off. This place was a zoo. If Mr. Memory doesn't watch it, he's going to get canned. He—"

"Harry," he said, with a gravity in his voice I'd never heard before. "I've got to see you right away."

"What's up?"

"I can't talk. You've got to get over here."

"Where?"

"My apartment." He gave me the address.

"What's wrong?"

"I can't talk. Just get your ass over here."

"Give me about an hour and—"

"No, now! You've got to come now."

"Jeez, Ed. You make it sound like a matter of life and death."

"It is. I can't tell you more, Harry. It isn't allowed. I want to tell you a story, but it's got be in person. Can you come now?"

It reminded me too much of Cate's phone call a couple of days ago. I took a breath and let it out in a frustrated sigh. "All right. I'll be there."

I hung up and Cate asked what was wrong. "I don't know. He wouldn't say."

"Another kidnapping?"

"Could be."

Cate looked down at the floor and said nothing. The pained puzzlement on her face reminded me of Hayden Miller wondering where the flowers went. I dumped my equipment into the trunk and peeled off my tux coat. As we rushed off, I tried to ignore the fact that I was walking into an unknown danger with nothing to defend myself but the magic wand in my pocket.

CHAPTER TWENTY-ONE

I knocked on McClenahan's door, and was greeted with the tinkle of breaking glass, the clunk of a chair overturning, and the sound of a woman weeping.

"Hurry," Cate said as I fumbled for my lock picks.

Just as I got them out, the door swung open. A lady wearing shorts that showed off her long tanned legs was standing in the doorway, a tall drink in her hand and a crooked grin on her face. Behind her a woman in an evening gown was tearfully mopping up the drink she had just dumped on her dress. Beside her on the hallway floor was the chair she had tripped over. A broken glass lay in a puddle at her feet.

" 'mon in," the woman with the shorts said, sounding as though she'd taken drinking lessons from Mr. Memory. "We've been expecting you . . . whoever the hell you are."

She drifted away, and Cate and I, exchanging wary glances, followed her inside, careful to sidestep the shards of glass. A man with a tray of plastic cups thrust two drinks into our hands. A blast of music erupted from a pair of Bose speakers mounted on pedestals in the living room, and the walls and floor shook with the beat.

"Do you see any emergency here?" I asked.

"Looks more like a party," Cate yelled.

The hallway and living room were crowded with guests who held drinks firmly in their hands. Some shouted to be heard over the music while others seemed to have given up any attempt at conversation and simply bobbed their heads to the rhythm. One couple was dancing in the hallway. In the corner of the living room stood a giant-screen TV, showing a cooking program hosted by someone called the "Canadian Chef." Sitting on the floor in front of the TV was one of the cooks from the Mystic Isle. He was cheering every move of the chef, as though he were watching a football game. I recognized a few of the other guests as members of the daytime staff of the Mystic Isle, but I didn't see McClenahan anywhere.

McClenahan's apartment was furnished with discarded props and set pieces from the movies, plays, and TV shows he had worked on. In the foyer was a space-station control console from a canceled science-fiction series. The sofa and love seat in the living room were covered with a rubber material that looked exactly like rock and had probably been used in a caveman movie. The rug was made of artificial football turf—impervious to spills, stains, and twenty-two-man pileups.

The centerpiece of the coffee table was a miniature fire truck, one of the special effects in a movie about a homicidal fire bug. The hallway leading from the living room ended at what was probably the bedroom door—a slab of melted, charred metal, presumably from a fictional nuclear blast.

Cate, afraid to sip the drink in her hand, looked around in awe of McClenahan's apartment-cum-prop closet. She stepped backwards until her shoulders bumped the wall. She turned and saw that it was coated with a plastic that gave the effect of a castle wall.

"Quite a collection, isn't it?" she said.

"It's a wonder this place isn't more cluttered. McClenahan used to work on *Comedy Live*, a network show that did over a dozen sketches per week. They used to crank the sets out so fast, the paint was often wet when they went on the air."

Although most of the partygoers seemed to be enjoying themselves, one man looked uneasy. He had a closely trimmed gray beard and wore a charcoal sports jacket with large flapped pockets decorated with chestnut-size buttons. Cate and I jostled our way through the crowd to his side.

Flakes of chopped ice still floated in his neglected drink, which he held stiffly in front of him. "Hello, Mr. Colderwood. Glad you could make it to Ed McClenahan's private little carnival."

I tried to place his face. "Let's see. I know you. You're, uh . . ."

"Strumpf. John Strumpf. I'm on retainer at the Mystic Isle."

"I remember now. You keep the books for Al Emmons."

"That right. It doesn't require much. I come in once a week and update the accounts. The main reason I took the job was because I love magic. My contract calls for free admission to all the shows. I'm glad you showed up tonight. With your grasp of the inexplicable, maybe you can figure out what the hell's going on."

I introduced him to Cate, and the three of us raised our glasses, each waiting for the others to taste the mysterious concoction. I turned out to be the brave one. Despite an unsavory taste like bad apple cider, an invigorating tingle crept down my throat and began to work its wonders. I tilted my glass back and took a bigger sip.

"All right, why don't you start?" I said to Strumpf. "What brings you out to a party at an apartment that looks like it was furnished by Ethan Allen's of Mars?"

"Ed McClenahan called me, sounding desperate. He said he needed help, but wouldn't say why. I rushed over here as quick as I could. Hell, my wife and I were spending a pleasant evening at home with a bag of popcorn and some rented movies."

"He used the same line on us," Cate said. "I wonder how many here received similar calls. Some look like they'd be ready for a party at the drop of a hat. But there are a few who look as ticked off as us. I bet they're sticking around to find out what's up."

I said, "The big question is, where's our host?"

As if in answer, the groan of rusty metal pierced through the pulsing stereo, sounding like a castle gate being lowered after a hundred years' disuse. It was the molten metal door to Mc-Clenahan's bedroom. I looked out in the hallway and recognized McClenahan standing there. He had treated his normally unkempt hair to a fifty-dollar salon treatment. It conformed to the contours of his head like landscaped shrubbery. He wore a white suit with a powder-blue vest, and a diamond-clustered pin gleamed from his lapel. Carrying an attaché case made from leather as rich as a show horse's saddle, McClenahan walked with a no-nonsense assurance I'd never seen in him before. He definitely wasn't playing the role of party host. Nor did I detect any of the urgency I'd heard in his phone call.

"Looks like he means business," Strumpf said.

He couldn't have been more accurate.

McClenahan strode over to the stereo and clicked it off in midsong. He set his attaché case on the seat of a chair, opened it, and took out a metal frame that resembled a music stand. After unfolding the frame and setting it on the floor, he reached behind the couch for a set of flip charts, which he set on his easel.

He took an aluminum stick from his case and expanded it like a car antenna. As he cleared his throat, I noticed that the couple who had been dancing in the hallway were now standing in the corner, arms wrapped around each other, kissing.

"Ladies and gentlemen," McClenahan said. "Thank you so much for coming." He paused so that the couple in the corner would realize that he was about to have a momentous effect on their lives, but they were more interested in other things momentous. After a moment McClenahan continued. "How many of you wish there was a magic way to stretch your paychecks at the end of the week?"

No one raised his hand. As McClenahan continued, Strumpf swore to himself and began reciting McClenahan's words along with him. Apparently, Strumpf had been to another party like this.

"How many of you have ever heard of a company called Renaissance, Inc.?" Strumpf and McClenahan said in unison.

Many in the crowd groaned. They, too, had been similarly shanghaied before.

Sounding like a third-grader reciting in a church play, McClenahan said, "I'd like to share with you the wonder of the Renaissance story."

Strumpf downed the rest of his drink. Taking my empty glass he said, "So it won't be a total loss, how about one for the road?"

plenish lost body fluid. I blinked, and the image of Ed Mc-
Clenahan split and drifted apart.

"I need some air." I handed Cate my glass and stepped through
the sliding door, out onto the balcony. Six floors up, the terrace
looked out on the sleeping town of Parrish. As house lights in the
distance blinked off, the low-lying buildings at the edge of town
blended in with the hills and mountains on the horizon. I gazed at
the flashing neon "M" on the roof of the Mystic Isle, several
blocks away. Beside the club loomed the hulking warehouse
that housed Al Emmons's illusions, to which my own would
soon be added. I knew that if I went crawling back to Emmons
and asked to buy everything back, it would cost at least forty
percent more than he paid me. Emmons wasn't a bad man, just
a good businessman.

"Business," I muttered sarcastically, glancing back through
the glass at McClenahan, who was still slogging through his talk.
Despite his clumsy presentation, I grudgingly admired the style
of the sales pitch. Certain words and phrases were ingeniously
designed to stick with you, like well-written radio and TV jin-
gles.

I started to go back in when I stopped short, jolted by what I
saw. As I stared at the furniture on the balcony, six years of my
life were painfully stripped away.

My anger at McClenahan for tricking us suddenly dissipated.
"Ed," I said to myself, "you never said you worked on *that*
show."

In the corner sat a park bench. Beside it was a street lamp
with a sign marking the intersection of Maple Avenue and Third
Street. The bench was double-sized and the street lamp was tilted
at a nightmarish angle. They had been part of a setting for my
network special that had never aired. Ed McClenahan must have
been one of the property men for the show. The bench had been
used in a sketch where I levitated a gang of kids playing stick-
ball. Maple and Third were real streets near my boyhood home.

I sat down heavily on the bench, put my foot up on the balcony
railing, and watched the woolly clouds overtake and swallow the
moon. The sliding door shushed open and closed, and Cate was
standing on the balcony. A few moments later she was sitting
next to me.

In silence, I watched the breeze stir the tree branches down
below. I wished I could hit a magic button, like on McClenahan's

VCR, to freeze this moment in time. Then maybe Cate and I would have time to roll out from under the wheels of so-called justice that were bearing down on us. It would give us time to catch our breath, time to get to know each other again. Cate finished her drink and threw it over the railing. A few seconds later, the plastic cup thonked on the sidewalk and a voice yelled, "Hey!" Cate giggled.

"Realize what intersection we're at?" I asked.

She looked up at the sign and gasped. A sad look dimmed some of the light in her eyes, and I didn't like it. I put my arm around her in what began as a friendly caress but turned into a strong, clinging embrace. She didn't return my affection. I tilted her head back and kissed her gently, but she felt limp and distant. Just as I was about to apologize, she returned my kiss with an ardor that seemed almost a desperate plea.

McClenahan had created many alien worlds inside his apartment. But to me, this balcony wasn't strange at all. It was a piece of home. As Cate and I pulled each other close, I thought of the power of illusion. An illusion, conceived by a murderer bent on framing Cate, had brought her and me back together again. An illusion of emergency, created by McClenahan, had made us race to his apartment tonight. And now—at the intersection of Maple and Third—Cate and I were basking in the illusion that it was six years ago and a bright uncomplicated future lay ahead for both of us.

I kissed her again, but this time we were just going through the motions, as we did in the final days before she left for good. I pulled away from her and folded my hands on my lap. She sighed and slid to the end of the bench.

"What's wrong?" I asked. "First you're angry, as if I tricked you to come out on the balcony. Then you want to kiss me. Then you get angry all over again. Why?" But I knew what was wrong. Years can pass, but some things never change.

"I can see that single-minded, predatory look on your face, the one that means you're about to shut everything out of your life again . . . especially me. I know what that look means. You've stumbled onto something, haven't you?"

"As a matter of fact, I have. It's—"

"It doesn't matter *what* it is. I just can't help wondering if you're investigating this case to help me, or if it's just another challenge to crack a baffling illusion. Harry, it's that same old question again—what's more important, magic or me? Are you doing all this to help me, or to make a name for yourself and get back into the spotlight again?''

I pulled her toward me and tried my damnedest to prove that my feelings for her were stronger than for anything else in my life. I didn't do very well. Her lips remained cold and unresponsive.

I gave up and looked out over the balcony at the blinking red M. ''You're right. I do have an idea.''

I explained to her my plan, and how it had been inspired by McClenahan's bench and street post. When I finished, she said, ''So what's your next step?''

''You and I are going to sign up for Renaissance, Inc.''

''We're what?''

''After we've gained McClenahan's undivided attention, we're going to ask him to retrace the chain of sales reps leading up to his invitation to join the company.''

''What good will that do?''

I pulled out my notes on Posar's invitation to the poker game. ''Notice any similarity between this and McClenahan's talk tonight?''

Cate read the invitation and nodded. ''Hey, you're right. They both used the words 'cordially invite' and 'attractive stakes.' And they both requested that only first names to used. Do you think McClenahan is involved in the murder?''

''No way. I think that either the murderer subconsciously borrowed some of the wording for the invitation, or—''

''Or the murderer has a macabre sense of humor and deliberately used the words.''

''Exactly. It might be a good idea to contact Lester Zehme and ask him to check if any of the other suspects were ever involved with Renaissance, Inc.''

We both looked through the glass door. The number of guests had dwindled drastically, and McClenahan was now passing out applications for Renaissance, printed on computer cards. I didn't tell Cate that I had something else in mind besides tracing the names. Something slightly illegal.

I drew Cate close once again and tried to convince her that my motives weren't all professional. This time I made considerable progress.

CHAPTER TWENTY-THREE

The gossip column business must have been lucrative. The electronic security system on Lisa South's house was worth as much as the average home in Parrish. But despite the expense, it wasn't worth a dime right now because it wasn't turned on. Either the police couldn't figure out how to reset it or the murderer had permanently damaged it the night of his visit. After three minutes with my lock picks, I stepped through the rear entrance, without a bip or a buzz or a recording that said *"Halt! The police have been notified!"*

The air conditioning was on, but it wasn't adjusted properly. It was baking inside, as if the violence that visited here had made the air hard to breathe; a grim reminder of death's finality. The first place I searched was the kitchen. There were no personal touches—no humorous refrigerator magnets or novelty pot holders. There was hardly any food in the cupboards and refrigerator, and only a few cooking appliances and utensils. Lisa South had probably dined out most of the time, hiring a caterer when she had guests.

I moved into the living room, the murder scene. The design on the rug in the middle of the room was a delicate tangle of vines and flowers and plumed birds. The whimsical pattern was marred by an oval blotch of dark red at one end. I knelt, and it was several seconds before I could bring myself to touch the spot. Even though the blood was dry, I still felt like running to the kitchen and holding my fingers under scalding water. I stood up and moved away from the rug, reminding myself that I wasn't here to dig up physical evidence. Like vultures at mealtime, the police would have picked this place clean, gathering all sorts of minute samples for lab analysis.

No, I was hoping to find something that the cops—unaware of Ali Zehme and the four poker-playing suspects—had overlooked. I wandered aimlessly, feeling like a prospective buyer touring a house with the owner away.

Dominating the living room was a life-size, realistic portrait of a man who'd have looked at home in a 1930s crime movie. He wore a wrinkled suit and a felt hat pulled over reddened eyes. Snarling, he held a lit cigarette in one hand and a smoking revolver in the other. He glared savagely at the blond woman on the floor whom he had just shot. In the lower corner of the picture was the signature of James Brittain, an artist noted more for his antiwar activism than his painting.

Nearly all the art in Lisa South's house had violent themes. Hanging next to the portrait of the gunman was a watercolor of two bare-knuckled prizefighters. Below that was a pen-and-ink of a young girl near death upon a dunking stool during the Salem witch-hunt era. Atop the television set were miniature Civil War cannons.

I sifted through end table drawers, flipped over cushions, and peeked under rugs and mats. Using a butter knife from the kitchen, I unscrewed the heating and air duct covers, and shoved my arm in as far as I could. I fanned through every book on the high shelves in the living room.

To say that Lisa South was security conscious was an understatement. She had made a second career of paranoia. The police had discovered and confiscated a variety of weapons, but not all of them. I found a tear-gas gun with an old expiration date clipped to the inside of a drapery rod on the front window. I unscrewed the tip of an umbrella from a downstairs closet, exposing a three-inch sword tip with a razor edge. Upstairs, behind the panel that covered the water pipes of her shower, I discovered some loose floorboards. After ten sweaty minutes, I pulled away two of the boards and found a .38 Special. Not the murder weapon, however, which was a .45 caliber. I theorized that Lisa South's excessive caution was a by-product of her profession, that she feared that one of the unlucky victims of her avid reporting might someday go off the deep end.

I poked around in her closets and dresser drawers, wondering how policemen ever get used to fingering people's personal belongings. In one drawer was a certificate from an indoor pistol range in Beverly Hills, certifying that two years ago Lisa had completed a safe handgun course. A lot of good the training had done her the other night.

Going downstairs again, I entered the alcove next to her living room. It was a small study, equipped with a portable typewriter. With its cheery fireplace and gold-tinted walls, it was a place to relax, not work. I pulled a sheaf of papers from the zippered compartment in the typewriter case. Most were fan letters, but in the middle I found several letters from friends, urging her to write a series of columns about a business they claimed had defrauded them—Renaissance, Inc. I replaced the letters and zipped up the case. I found no files or notes or rough drafts. Apparently, Lisa South wanted to forget about work when staying at this house.

Careful to sidestep the stained rug, I went over and sat on the sofa. I looked out the bay window. A mile away across forested hills, barely visible, was the white roof of the Mount Pacific Resort. The blue water of its three swimming pools glistened in the distance. Cate had taken the job on the chorus line there to make some money before she resumed her acting career. Time was ticking inexorably away on both our careers. In a few years the only roles she'd be considered for would be character parts. I, too, would soon have to make changes in my stage persona. The role of the youthful, boy-magician no longer fit me, and I'd have to defer that character to Edward and the Dean Brothers. Not wanting to dwell on that unpleasant thought, I concentrated again on searching a dead woman's house—a role more suited for the gunman in the painting on Lisa South's wall.

Although my instincts told me I only lacked one piece to make the whole puzzle fit neatly together, I was sure that a further search of the house would yield little. I was tired and hungry, and my limbs felt oddly relaxed. As I stretched out my legs, my head dropped to the side, my ear brushing my shoulder. I bolted to my feet, chasing sleep away just as it was about to settle in for a long visit. I wanted to leave quickly, but decided to check the one place I had thus far avoided—the room where Cate had been held prisoner.

Lisa South's basement was primarily a storage area, with boxes stacked on wooden skids to avoid flood damage. I opened the wooden door in the corner and saw that Cate's temporary cell had once been a coal bin. I switched on the light and watched a spider do a quickstep across an old mattress in the middle of the floor. Along the side wall ran the pipe where Cate had been handcuffed.

As I turned off the light, I heard a bonking noise from upstairs, followed by a patter of feet. Two voices battled inside me. The coward in me pleaded with me to crouch in a dark corner and be thankful that I wasn't upstairs with the intruder. Another voice—the magician in me—wanted to catch a glimpse of the visitor.

The instinctive magician won, and he arrogantly vanished the coward in a puff of smoke. I advanced lightly to the top of the steps and opened the cellar door a fraction of an inch, knocking over the pots and pans heaped in front of it.

I heard someone slam a cupboard door and start running. More pans hit the floor. The house shook as the back door slammed. Through the kitchen window, I caught sight of a short man—shorter than any of the poker players, including Nikki—circling toward the front of the house at a speed I knew I couldn't match. He was dressed in black.

Most of the cupboard doors hung open. The intruder had also come to search the house. He had dragged the pans out onto the floor to get a better look inside the bottom row of cupboards. I picked up a black snap-brim hat lying on the floor beside the pans. There was no identification on the sweat band.

Using the kitchen phone, I dialed my hotel room and Cate answered.

"Harry," she said, "I have some good news. I talked to Lester Zehme, and as you suspected, Renaissance keeps a computer record of everyone who attends introductory sales meetings. Zehme asked his main office to do a search on all the poker players. In the past three years each of them has attended a Renaissance meeting. None of them, however, expressed interest in joining the company."

"Didn't Zehme think it strange they had all attended meetings?"

"Not really. He said that due to the mild trickery in luring people to those meetings, a wide variety of people have been exposed to his company's message."

"What about the fact that none of them recognized Zehme as the founder of Renaissance?"

"Zehme pointed out that he values his privacy. Just as he's

kept his picture out of the newspapers, he's never had it printed in any company brochures.''

''So what's the other good news, Cate?''

''I traced back the line of sales reps that led up to McClenahan being recruited into Renaissance. I felt 'like an epidemiologist tracking down a disease.''

''In a sense, maybe you were.''

''I found out that several of the Mystic Isle staff have recently gotten involved in the company.''

''And who signed *them* up?''

''All their memberships stem from one man. His name's Jerome Longley.''

''Who's he?''

''A chauffeur for a local limousine service.''

I snapped my fingers. Of course, the driver that took us to the poker game. He was the missing link.

I squeezed the black hat in my hand. A chauffeur's hat.

CHAPTER TWENTY-FOUR

I showed the owner of Carriage Limo Leasing a business card that said I was from a credit bureau. I told him that I was checking into a loan problem of one of his drivers—Jerome Longley. Truth was, the card had been given to me by an investigator who was looking into a financial problem of mine. The owner let me look through his files. I found a photo of Longley and a copy of his license, but nothing else. All the owner could tell me about Longley was that he was a neat, conscientious employee whom he trusted. Longley took such good care of his vehicle that the owner often let him use it outside of work. I wrote down Longley's address and decided to visit him. Then I called Cate and told her what time to meet me there.

When Longley didn't answer my knock, I went down to the store below his apartment—a convenience store whose location had recently become quite inconvenient, due to the rerouting of a nearby highway. The business was failing miserably. The owner, Mrs. Harriet O'Brien, was a bony woman in her late sixties. She was dressed in a cardigan sweater, too warm for the humid day. She sat on a wicker chair, smoking a cigarette and looking as if she was merely marking time until her business fell to pieces. On the day she finally closed for good, if she didn't slam the door too hard, the ramshackle building just might stand long enough for the wrecking ball to do its work.

While I waited for Cate to arrive, Mrs. O'Brien and I made small talk about good weather and bad weathermen. As the minutes dragged by, she grew steadily more suspicious, but she didn't say anything. When Cate finally showed up—forty-five minutes late—she gave no explanation for her tardiness. Mrs. O'Brien immediately ignored me and started eyeing Cate, both for her beauty and in wonder of why we—strangers to the neighbor-hood—were visiting her store now that the new highway had taken it so far off the beaten path.

I asked Mrs. O'Brien about Jerome Longley.

"I never had trouble with Jerome," she said, peeling down the wrapper of a chocolate bar in sections like a banana. She took off a third of it in one bite. "He pays his rent on time and he's discreet about entertaining lady friends." Her eyes sparkled. "If I were a few decades younger, perhaps he'd try to sweet-talk me upstairs too. Let me tell you, I'd have gladly gone. I like him. Of course, I've never seen him in the company of anyone as pretty as your young lady here."

Cate smiled in thanks and wandered to the magazine rack where she began leafing though a magazine featuring "winning" lottery numbers based on the interpretation of dreams.

"How long has Jerome been a chauffeur?" I asked.

"A couple years. With so many rich folks with summer homes in town, a local limo service opened up a while back and has done quite well. I hear the owner now has eight of those big cars he rents out constantly."

"Is Jerome at work now?"

"No, Friday's his day off."

Mrs. O'Brien excused herself to wait on a man who bought a quart of milk and fifteen dollars in lottery tickets. When he left, she said, "Jerome was a cabby for five years, but he says he makes more money now without the hassle of hustling for tips. The only bad thing, he says, is that a chauffeur has to put up with a lot of guff—believe me, 'guff' wasn't the word he used—from the wealthy folks he drives for. To tell the truth, I think he likes his handsome little uniform. Not long after he started wearing it, he began to have better luck with his lady visitors. Jerome is such a short man, I think it made him look taller. I guess there'll always be the type who go for men in uniforms."

"Do you think any of his 'visitors' were the wives of his limo clients?"

She threw away her candy wrapper and grabbed a bag of mixed nuts from the shelf behind her. "Could be. I never got nosy and asked."

I bought a pack of Luckies and started stripping off the wrapper. Even though I had seen her smoking before, I hesitated before shaking out a cigarette. "It's okay. Go ahead," she said.

"I don't smoke as heavy as I used to, but I still enjoy one now and then. Now, Jerome is a different story—an unrepentant chain smoker." Mrs. O'Brien dumped her nuts into a paper plate and started eating the cashews first, carefully choosing which teeth to chew them with. "Whoever Jerome's been making time with lately must think she's too high-class to come to his place."

"Oh, yeah?"

"You see, I have a gentleman friend of my own." Mrs. O'Brien must not have liked the way Cate grinned, because she quickly added, "Strictly aboveboard, I'll have you know. I'm a widow and he's never been married. We only go out twice a week. Anyway, my friend and I like to take early evening drives. More than a few times, we've seen Jerome driving his limo on the old Artwick road. I know it's Jerome because he's the only driver who wears the cap with his uniform. Every time we saw him, he was always too far ahead, going too fast for us to see who was in the car with him."

"Artwick Road?"

"It's the third turn off the highway leading east out of town. It's a popular lover's lane." This time Cate didn't even get a chance to smile before Mrs. O'Brien said, "Young lady, if you must know, my friend and I go there to pick berries and look at the wildflowers. Very pretty this time of the year. And we *always* leave before dark." After finishing of the rest of her nuts, she said, "Why are you so interested in Jerome?'

"Cate and I are reporters, doing a feature on people with unusual occupations. We'll be in town for a few more days. When you see Jerome, tell him to call me"—I wrote my name on a slip of paper—"at the Spears Hotel."

Mrs. O'Brien gave Cate a sidelong glance, apparently unable to believe that she'd stay at a place like the Spears.

"How about putting me in your story, too?" Mrs. O'Brien said. "I've got an unusual occupation."

"You do?"

"Sure. Ever meet anyone that earns a living selling only milk, bread, baseball cards, and lottery tickets? Anymore, that's ninety percent of my business."

I laughed, and she promised to pass my message on to Longley. Cate put her dream-and-lottery magazine back on the rack, next to a tabloid newspaper that printed celebrity news ten times

sleazier than Lisa South's column. As I started out the door, Cate
said, "Wait a minute."

She dug in her purse and pulled out several dollar bills. She
opened the magazine again and read off a number, asking Mrs.
O'Brien to punch it into her Lotto machine. After paying for the
tickets, Cate taunted me by fanning them in front of my face
before she tucked them away in her purse.

Outside, I said, "I can't believe you bought that garbage.
Didn't all those years of working with me have any effect? What's
next? Are you going to spend the evening with a palm reader?"

"Hey, I didn't do anything so blasphemous. All I did was bet
on the number that the magazine recommended, based on a
dream I had last night."

"What kind of dream?"

"Oh, it's embarrassing to talk about. It's a little racy. . . ."
Cate explained that the only people in her dream were her and
me. She then went into such explicit detail that I was glad we
were out of Mrs. O'Brien's earshot. When she finished, I found
myself wishing there were more, that she had dreamed a little
longer. I said, "Any chance you believe in dreams coming true?"

"No, not by themselves. They usually need a little help from
the people who dream them."

"And in your case . . . ?"

Cate gave an enigmatic smile but she didn't answer. I decided
not to press my luck. There'd be time enough this evening to
continue our discussion of dream fulfillment.

As we got into the van she asked, "Where are we going now?"

"Where else? Lover's Lane."

She started to get out, pretending to be outraged. "So much
for sharing my innermost thoughts with you!"

"No, wait. We're just going there to pick berries, and look at
the wildflowers. I promise we'll leave before dark."

Laughing, Cate got back in and shut the door. I turned on the
radio, hoping to hear today's lottery number and prove her folly
with the dream book. As Cate slid closer, I picked up Longley's
cap and pitched it to the back of the van. Its touch made my skin
feel shriveled.

"I saw something black," Cate said suddenly. "Back on that
side road."

I tapped the brakes and the van slid over the gravel before

stopping abruptly. Because of deep ditches on both sides, I had to take three cautious backups to reverse direction.

"Which side of the road?" I asked. There was a whole network of unpaved offshoots along Artwick Road.

"Things look different from this direction. Wait. There. Go back that way."

I jerked the wheel to the left, and the van bounced over the rocks and chuckholes in the new road. Boxes of magic equipment rattled in the back. I slowed to a crawl, not wanting to damage my van, which had lately declared a truce in terms of repair bills. I slowed even more as the road withered away, leaving us at the edge of a clearing.

I came to a stop when I realized that the flash of black Cate had seen through the bushes and trees was indeed a limousine. It was parked at the other end of the clearing. The engine was off. The windows were dark, preventing a view inside.

"Stay here," I said.

"What's that sticking out the back? Is that a—?"

I knew from the catch in her voice that she had figured out, as I had, what was attached to the rear of the black car. I turned off my engine and listened for a moment. The air was still, quieter than I'd imagined it would be. I left my door open and took my time approaching the limo, listening for any change in the wind jostling the trees. Flies buzzed around my face and slapping at them did no good. My heels squished in the marshy ground.

The hose on the back of the limo had been cut from an old vacuum cleaner. One end was attached to the exhaust pipe, and the other was shoved through the front window, which was wound up tight against the hose. Feeling as though an automatic pilot was guiding my body, I walked stiffly to the passenger side and looked in.

Through the dark glass I saw a man slumped across the front seat. I recognized Jerome Longley from the picture on his license at the limo service. His eyes were open and were staring at the radio with mild displeasure, as though he didn't like the station it was tuned to. I guess they didn't draw his lottery number today, I thought grimly. A short, trim man in his early forties, Longley was wearing a white shirt, a black coat and trousers, but no hat. The perfect shine of his shoes caught the sunlight. Even the soles and sides of the heels were black with polish.

I looked back at Cate. She showed no signs of getting out of the van to share in a sight she'd forever regret—one that was going to be hard to wipe from my own memory.

I took a deep breath and opened the passenger door. Warm, moist air escaped, wrapping sickeningly around me, then drifting off in the breeze. I placed my two fingers on Longley's neck but I couldn't find a pulse. His skin was hot, reminding me of an overripe vegetable left in the sun. I stepped back out of the car and tilted my head up, soothing my burning eyes with the view of clean clouds in a deep blue sky. I waited for my labored breathing to calm down and for the sudden feeling of nausea to pass.

I stuck my head back into the car again. Steeling myself against a rush of wooziness, I let my eyes roam over the rest of the car. The keys were still in the ignition and the ashtray was brimming with butts. The filters were all facing me. Except for the ashtray and a strip of dust that extended a few inches around the base of the front seat, the interior of the car was immaculate. I rubbed my finger along the mat and it came away clean. I allowed myself a weak smile and thought, "Try that on the floor of my van and you'll be lucky to come away with your own finger."

I closed the door, leaving Longley alone to wait for the police to show up and cordon off the area. They'd comb the clearing, take their pictures, jot their notes, search in vain for a suicide note, and then disperse to talk to Longley's friends, half of whom would probably express disbelief while the other half would say yes, they had seen the tragedy coming. Poor Jerome has been so dejected lately.

I knocked the mud off my shoes, crawled back into the van, and sped back toward the highway without a word. Cate wore a worried expression, gasping as she slid from side to side, alternately bumping up against me and the door. Boxes behind us tumbled to the floor.

At the sound of shattering glass, she looked at me sharply. I said, "Don't worry. If anything's broken, I'll send it to Al Emmons, along with all the rest of my illusions."

I ground to a stop several feet before the road met the highway. Not wanting any witnesses to see me pull out of Artwick Road, I waited until the highway was completely empty. Then I swung onto the paved road where I immediately adopted a saner driving style.

I told Cate what I'd seen in the limo and explained to her what I thought it all meant.

"Do we call the police?" she asked.

"I think an anonymous tip would be best. After that, we're going to strike a deal with Mrs. Harriet O'Brien, watch a little TV, take a few pictures, and then go knock on some doors."

In addition, I was going to call the reference section of the local library. I had a history question that badly needed answering.

CHAPTER TWENTY-FIVE

I once answered an ad in *Boy's Life* magazine. The picture in the ad was crammed with enticing prizes: bikes, record players, radios, and model planes. "All this—and more—can be yours if you know only twenty-five people in your neighborhood!" was the promise. The ad neglected to say that you also had to persuade those twenty-five people to buy garden seeds . . . lots and lots of seeds. Even though I never sold any seeds, I did receive a cheap baseball mitt from the seed company. Suffice it to say, my parents had one hell of a garden that year.

I was still thinking about all those unsold seeds as Cate and I knocked on doors in Lisa South's neighborhood. After phoning in an anonymous tip to the police about Jerome Longley, we'd gone back to the Mystic Isle to rerun Milan Posar's music video on the VCR. As the camera did a long pan of the empty game room, I'd taken a picture of the TV screen. We'd gotten the film developed at a one-hour processor.

Working opposite sides of the street, Cate and I canvassed every house within five minutes of Lisa South's home. It took the better part of two hours to complete our survey.

When we'd finished, we sat on a curb two houses down from the South home. Nearby lawn mowers sounded like low-flying aircraft. I looked at Lisa South's front lawn. It already showed neglect. Long blades of grass swayed in the breeze.

"Think we missed any houses?" I asked.

"No way. I only found five houses where no one was home. In each case, I found a neighbor who had been inside the house in question."

"And?"

"They all said they didn't know of a game room in the neighborhood that matched the one in our pictures."

"Same here." Our story was simple: Cate and I had posed as salesmen for a home remodeler. As an example of our fine work, we showed pictures of the game room in the video. We gauged reactions carefully, and none of the people acted suspicious or indicated that any of their neighbors had such a room in their basements. The most frequent reply was *Oh, sure, I know plenty of people with similar game rooms, but none that look exactly like that.*

"My feet are killing me," Cate said. "I bet yours are too. And you still have a show to do tonight."

"I have an even more important performance to prepare for. There are still a few things I'm not quite sure of. Why don't we talk about it over dinner? We'll find a nice cheap restaurant . . . one with a pay phone."

"Pay phone?"

"I'm going to call someone to do a stakeout for us."

"I could do the stakeout. I still have a little energy left."

"No, it's no job for us. We'd be recognized."

"Then who?"

"I know someone who'll gladly help. Harriet O'Brien."

When we got to the restaurant, I called Mrs. O'Brien. I stopped pretending to be a reporter and told her the truth, gently breaking the news about Jerome Longley. I then asked her a favor.

Cate and I were picking at the remains of our dessert when I thought it was time to check back on Mrs. O'Brien. She answered her phone and said in a tear-choked voice to wait until she took care of a customer. Long after the bells on her cash register died, I heard her blowing her nose and talking quietly to herself. A man picked up the pay phone on my right and I said to him, "Sorry. That one's busted. The last guy lost six quarters." He moved to the next one.

Back on the line, Mrs. O'Brien said, "I thought that guy would never leave. Six loaves of bread, two quarts of milk, and ten Lotto tickets . . . all with different numbers. What a pain." I heard her strike a match. "I keep asking myself why Jerome did such a ghastly thing to himself. I just don't see how I can help."

"Let me be the judge."

"Where do I start?"

"Just tell me what you saw."

"Okay. Let me warn you that it doesn't make much sense. After you called the first time, I closed up and drove to where you said. I didn't last long. If I treated my customers the way I was treated, I'd have been out of business thirty years ago."

I cleared my throat. "So what happened?"

"Let me get my notes." Her conscientious detective work made me smile.

"Okay. Here goes." She adopted the clinical tone of a policeman testifying in court. "At seven-thirty I parked my car where you told me. I didn't see anything for about thirty-five minutes. Then a goon stepped out of a garage in the alley and—"

"A goon?"

"What else can I call him? He was about six-three and weighed a good two-fifty. He hadn't shaved in days, and his shirt was two sizes small. When his type comes into my store, my hand stays on the pistol under my counter. I was ready to tail him, thinking he was going to mail the cardboard box under his arm. But he set it down and pulled a drum off the back of a pickup truck."

"Like a bass drum?"

"Hell, no. I mean an oil drum. An empty one. He got a hammer and a big nail, and pounded holes in it. He set the barrel on some bricks and dropped the cardboard box inside. He squirted lighter fluid in the barrel. I could smell the fumes even where I was."

"Any idea what was in the box?"

"Hold on, I'm coming to that." Her register chimed and she said thank you to a customer. "This guy tossed a match in the barrel, watched it burn a few seconds, and then returned to the garage. When the goon didn't come back, I sneaked over. Before I got close, the goon stormed out of the garage, calling me names a gentleman in my day would never call a lady. He said I was trespassing. I returned to my car and drove away, but I came back in twenty minutes. The goon was nowhere around. The fire had died down, so I broke a branch off a nearby tree and poked it around inside. There wasn't much left."

She paused to punch the cash register again. I wondered if she really had a customer, or if she just enjoyed keeping me in suspense. Finally, she said, "All that was left were some scraps of cloth, a metal zipper, and some melted buttons."

"That's it?"

"Yep. If none of this helps, I'll understand if you don't keep your part of the bargain . . ."

The image of Mrs. O'Brien holding a red-hot zipper at the end of a stick amused me. "No, you did fine. Expect a phone call soon from a man with the Mom and Pop's Corporation. They're going to evaluate your store to see if it's feasible to buy you out." I neglected to add that in return I had accepted the P.R. man's offer for me to promote—on a trial basis—the opening of two dozen new Mom and Pop's Stores. I cringed at the thought of dressing up like a crotchety old man, wearing a straw hat, smoking a pipe, and passing out balloons.

I looked across the restaurant to where Cate was thoughtfully swirling a spoon in her coffee. As I hung up, the phone on my right rang and I answered it. It was the reference librarian from the Parrish Public Library, returning my call. She said she'd assembled the information I'd requested on Nathan Hardan, the man who had pioneered the kind of pyramid scam that Renaissance, Inc., had honed to an art. I thanked her and she said, "Not at all. It was fascinating."

"Why's that?"

"When you first called, I wasn't sure I'd heard of Hardan before. After doing some reading, I vaguely remembered my parents speaking reverently of him when I was a child. He was apparently a well-respected national figure at one time. It wasn't until years after his death that Hardan's reputation went sour. Had he still been alive, it would have been a huge scandal. The charities he'd founded were discovered to be laundering money for his crooked businesses. Hardan was also suspected of killing two of his three mistresses. One of his wives had disappeared without a trace. By spreading money around in the right places, he kept the cases out of court. Hardan's main obsession in life was his fear that his fame would be fleeting. Since nowadays nobody seems to have heard of him, those fears were well-founded, weren't they?"

"Maybe, maybe not," I said. I thanked her and hung up.

When I returned to our table Cate commented that her feet were starting to recover from pounding the pavement. I answered with a nod, but my mind was elsewhere. As I picked at my cherry pie with my fork, I recalled the time my parents took me to Gettysburg when I was eleven. Though it was a hot day, touring the battlefields gave me a chill. There'd been no boyhood romanticism about war for me. My parents were disappointed that the only thing I enjoyed was a wax museum. My favorite exhibit was covered with a paint-spattered canvas. The sign said *Men at Work.* Lifting a canvas flap, I looked into a room filled with men in hats, T-shirts, and jeans, painting the walls. After a few seconds I realized they were all wax dummies—a practical joke on the overly curious. In their own way, the wax artists had tried to counteract the oppressive atmosphere of death that hung over the other war exhibits.

As I reflected on lifting that canvas, I realized where the poker game had been played. "Cate," I said, speaking too loudly and abruptly. She stared at her reflection in the coffee, not wanting to look up. She had heard me talk like this before and never liked the results. "I need a magic assistant."

"Uh-uh. No way. Those days are long gone."

"No, this is only for a short time."

"Not a chance."

"It's for just one trick. Let me explain . . ."

As I laid out my plan, her coffee grew cold. I noticed that she had slipped her shoes back on again and she no longer looked exhausted.

Good. There was plenty of work ahead.

CHAPTER TWENTY-SIX

None of the performers at the Mystic Isle questioned what I was doing. They were used to the eccentric behavior of their colleagues. I was stretching a tape measure along the floor in front of the double doors of the tunnel leading to Al Emmons's warehouse. As I jotted the measurements on my notepad, I heard the MC on the wall speaker invite Edward back onstage for another bow. Applause drowned out his voice. I took out my tie-clasp camera and began snapping pictures.

"Shall I say 'cheese'?" Mr. Memory said, walking out of his dressing room and in front of my camera. The glass in his hand contained a caramel-colored liquid.

"Just the man I want. I hate to bring it up, but how are the old brain cells this evening?"

He smiled and drained the last of his drink, careful not to dislodge the ice chunks at the bottom. "This is just diet soda. I'm out of my brain-pickling cycle for now. I'll be good for a month or so . . . until something sends me into another tailspin."

"What caused the last one?"

"It didn't take much. While waiting for a bus on a street corner, I heard two men arguing. After a few minutes, they ran out of steam and apologized to each other. As they got on the bus, one of them said something that really tore me up."

"What was that?"

"He patted his friend on the back and said, 'Forget about it.' Harry, I'd pay a million dollars to be able to do that."

I nodded in sympathy and handed him an envelope full of pictures. When he looked inside, he said, "I already saw these."

"I know, but I'd like you to try something different. It'll only take a few minutes. Here."

With a black marking pen, I demonstrated what I wanted him to do. "Don't worry about ruining them," I said. "I have plenty of copies. Why don't you go into your dressing room and get comfortable?"

Mr. Memory seemed intrigued, like a child learning a new game, and began using the marking pen on his way to his dressing room. Although he didn't understand what difference the pen could make, I knew it was necessary. Mr. Memory's mind was totally literal. He once tried to join an organization of people with genius IQs, but he failed their test. Furious, he attended one of their meetings uninvited. After the reading of the minutes, Mr. Memory stood up and recited them verbatim. When ordered to shut up, he recited them *backwards*. The president and vice-president—with IQs totaling well over three hundred fifty—forcibly ejected him. Mr. Memory's brand of mind power didn't impress them.

I was measuring the casing around the wall speaker when Cate came slowly down the steps. The enthusiasm she'd felt this afternoon had obviously worn off. She was an hour late but she gave me no excuse. She sat on the bottom step and rested her forehead on her crossed arms. "Shouldn't you clear all this with Al Emmons?"

I flicked the metal tape and it zipped back inside its case. "Think about it for a minute, Cate. Why do we need permission?"

She looked up and said, "Yeah, you're right. What was I thinking of?"

She watched as I silently reviewed the figures on my notepad. When I was done, she handed me a stack of brochures from her purse. "Will they be enough?"

I unfolded one. It was a pamphlet about the Mystic Isle that Al Emmons had printed up for tourist bureaus. "Perfect. We'll only need four. Is Roberta done with the letters?"

"Yes, she's got the master copy typed into her word processor, ready to print one out for each person."

"And what did the courier service say?"

"Since it's Friday, they can easily make their deliveries by late this evening. If it were a Saturday or Sunday, there might be trouble. Of course, they won't guarantee delivery to Jack Sullivan because he doesn't have a permanent address."

I handed her a slip of paper. "Here's a list of bars in town. If the couriers leave a message at each, saying they're holding a letter for Jack—one that might contain money—it'll bring him out of the woodwork fast. Now, what about the limos?''

"All taken care of. Are you sure you can pay for all this? I'll be glad to help . . ."

I waved off her offer.

"What about James Brittain, the painter?" I asked.

"I telephoned him. He had just returned from an anti-nuclear demonstration. He told me that his political and social views are always reflected in his art. No violence, *ever.*"

"That's what I thought."

"One more thing," she said. "There was a call from Nikki Beacham. She says she checked with some of her business associates about one of their steady customers. She wants you to call her back."

I wrote down Nikki's name and said, "I'll get hold of her later. Before we go any further, I'd better have my talk with Ed McClenahan." I put a quarter in the pay phone and dialed his apartment. Waiting for him to answer, I said, "Ed is heavily into the Renaissance company. He called off work again—the second night in a row."

Cate shook her head. "He'll get fired if he doesn't watch out."

"He's not worried. A guy with his talent won't have trouble finding work. Besides, what's a crummy job compared with the untold millions he'll earn with Renaissance?"

A man's voice answered and I heard talking and laughter in the background. Another Renaissance rally. I asked for McClenahan, and the man said McClenahan was busy "testifying," the Renaissance term for roping more suckers into their scheme.

"Tell him it's an emergency." Why not? I thought. The line had worked fine for McClenahan.

The man clunked down the phone. For five minutes, I listened to McClenahan's thin voice run through the same talk we'd heard the other night. A woman picked up the receiver and I asked for Ed. "Ed who?" she said.

In the distance, McClenahan said, "Don't hang up, Emily. It might be someone wanting to sign up." In a few moments he came on the line.

I identified myself and said, "Cate and I have given deep thought to what you said the other night about—"

"About voyaging to the stars of success? About mining life's gold before the golden years rob you?"

"Yeah. Something like that. In fact, I was so moved, I think you and I should go into business."

"Hot diggity! I knew you'd come around. I'll put together a packet of literature for you. Harry, with your performing ability, you'll be a natural. You'll hit the level of Master Renaissance Man in no time."

"Master Renaissance Man?"

"Sure. That entitles you to a whole slew of privileges, including exclusive classes at a special training facility."

"Ed, I hate to break this to you, but I'm still as utterly disgusted with Renaissance as before. Oh, perhaps you're right. If I gave it a shot, maybe I could move quickly up the ranks. But I already have a job fooling people. The big difference is that when people leave my shows, their checkbook balances are the same as when they walked in. No, Ed, the business proposition I have in mind is a limited one—we'll be partners for only one day. But it's honest work, involving something you're good at."

I offered him the money left over from making Cate's bail, plus my advance from the publicity campaign for the Mom and Pop's stores. Ed turned me down cold. It was chilling how his conversational tone now had the sing-song patter of his Renaissance sales pitch. "Ed, there are a few things you should know about Renaissance."

"Believe me, Harry, I'm well versed on the arguments against the company. For years there's been a smear campaign by well-meaning but ill-informed people."

Since I didn't have the time or money to hire a cult deprogrammer for McClenahan, I resorted to quick, brutal tactics.

"Ed, I have some arguments you *haven't* heard before."

"Go ahead. Shoot. I'm waiting."

I talked fast. At first he tried to interrupt, but his halfhearted protests gave way to stony silence. Fifteen minutes later, his voice weak, he agreed to help. He refused to be paid for his services, asking only for enough money to cover expenses.

After I hung up, Mr. Memory came storming out of his dressing room. His cheek was smudged with ink. Smiling triumphantly, he waved one of the photos. "Success, Harry. Success."

"Did you recognize one of the faces?"

"Yes."

"Do you remember the name?"

"Of course. Nathan Hardan."

CHAPTER TWENTY-SEVEN

I lugged my valise full of tricks to the bottom of the steps and surveyed the scene. I liked what I saw. The basement area was deserted. All the dressing room doors were closed. Other than the growl of distant thunder and the rain pelting against the building, the only sound was the waltz music of Edward's act wafting from the wall speaker. The violins were shriller than usual.

I flexed my fingers and they felt dry and filmy. There was still a trace of soap under my fingernails. I set my case down on a folding chair and began resetting my show. I ribbon-folded silk handkerchiefs and carefully poked them into dye tubes, hoping they'd last a few more shows before needing to be ironed. I sifted through the piles of playing cards, throwing away the damaged ones. I stacked them so that for my next show they'd be ready to conceal under my coat, where I could palm them out. I usually worked quickly while resetting but tonight I took my time, even dawdling. But it was okay.

I touched my forehead. It was only slightly damp. After a show I was usually drenched. That was okay, too.

Edward's music wavered underneath the roar of applause. I looked over at the portrait of Griffin Page, the first famous magician to play the Mystic Isle. I touched my forefinger to my brow in a sly salute. He continued to stare at me imperiously through thick spectacles.

Hearing a stirring in the tunnel behind the double doors, I set down my billiard balls and the black tubular bag I was loading them into. I crossed the room and heaved the plank off the doors, flinging it to the floor. It seemed lighter than the other day.

After pulling open the doors, I saw a flashlight bobbing at the other end of the tunnel. I heard Cate say, "Better not touch the walls. There's a mildew problem down here."

A female voice oohed in disgust, and I heard several padding footsteps. I flicked the light switch that illuminated my end of the tunnel.

A few seconds later five figures emerged from the blackness. Cate was in the lead, playing tour guide. Everyone shielded their eyes from the light pouring through the entrance.

As they came through the doorway, I motioned them toward the row of folding chairs and the couch arranged in the middle of the basement. The group looked dazed and disoriented, as if brimming with so many questions they didn't know where to start. And that was also okay by me.

One by one, they all found seats. First, Jack Sullivan—who looked as though he hadn't slept in two days—and then Nikki Beacham and Lester Zehme. The last to sit down was Milan Posar. He stared at the rows of dressing room doors, the pile of mattresses stacked beneath the overhead trap door, and the picture of Griffin Page, as if trying to remember where he'd seen them before.

"So *this* is where we are," he said, pulling a wrinkled pamphlet from his pocket. "The basement of that magic nightclub." He pointed at the pictures on the back of Al Emmons's tourist pamphlet. "Colderwood, I should have known you were behind all this when we got out of our limos and that Cate broad greeted us. What kind of place is that at the other end of the tunnel? Wait, I think I remember." He consulted the pamphlet again. "It's that warehouse where Emmons stores his magic illusions, isn't it? I wondered why all those big pretty boxes were stacked up." Posar laughed, proud of figuring this out. The others were less amused.

Last night, a courier had delivered envelopes to all of them. Each had contained the pamphlet and an invitation to play in a high-stakes poker game.

Jack, an unlit cigar between his teeth, was already preparing for what he hoped would be a profitable evening. He took out a deck of cards and started riffle-shuffling them, occasionally executing a practiced waterfall shuffle. Lester Zehme, wearing a baggy, open-necked shirt and plaid pants, looked as if he was ready to tee off at the country club. His hands were calmly folded on his lap. After spotting the flip charts behind me—with the

Renaissance coat of arms in the corner—he slid a leather case from his shirt pocket and put on a pair of clear-framed eyeglasses.

Nikki Beacham sat alone on the dusty old sofa, trying to look at ease. After closing the tunnel doors, Cate went over to my valise and pulled out a small cardboard box encased in shrinkwrap plastic. She gave Nikki a disdainful stare and moved to the far side of the flip charts. Reveling in Cate's glare, Nikki crossed and uncrossed her legs. She smiled as the eyes of the males in the room strayed in her direction.

I said good evening to everyone, but no one returned the greeting. "Life is short," I said. "Too short to be wasted chasing dollars. Yet most of us think we're hopelessly stuck at our present incomes. How untrue. I only ask you to keep an open mind as you listen to my concept of—"

I reached for the flip chart, shrugged, and simply waved a finger at it. The front sheet slowly rose by itself and flipped itself over the back, revealing, in giant bright letters, the words "THE HARRY COLDERWOOD ABRACADABRA PARTY PLAN."

I broadened my smile and talked so fast my words nearly jumped the tracks from my brain to my tongue. "Tired of the old nine-to-five grind?" I looked at Nikki, wearily studying her fingernails, and added: "Or the old eight P.M. to three A.M. grind? Then I recommend the Abracadabra Party Plan. It's the ideal way to combat boredom and also insure your financial future. With Abracadabra, you don't sell a product; you sell yourself—the most valuable product you have. As you concentrate on organizing parties, sharing our ideas with your friends, you will rapidly build a money-making empire of your own. Our product virtually sells itself."

Posar was eyeing the stairway intently. For a moment I thought he might attempt a hasty exit, but he turned and squinted at the box in Cate's hand. He said, "And exactly what product is going to make us all jillionaires?"

"Glad you asked . . . so glad you asked," I said in a carnival barker's drawl. I waved a magic wand at the chart. The first sheet—the one already flipped over the back—started to rise in the air. "Whoops. This thing's in reverse." I flicked an invisible switch at the end of the wand and shook it near my ear, as I would a broken watch. "There."

I waved it again and the front sheet jerkily doubled itself over the back to reveal the next sheet, which said "BOX O' TWO HUNDRED TRICKS."

Using my wand as a pointer, I slapped the charts so hard I nearly knocked over the easel. "A magician on TV usually does only a few tricks. But this little box contains a hundred times that many . . . at a cost of just a few dollars. My company will revolutionize the marketing of little magic sets. The days of answering tiny magic company ads in boys' magazines will be over. Magic sets will no longer be condemned to the toy sections of department stores. The glamorous world of magic is for everyone—kids and adults. Soon, *everyone* will have the opportunity to be the life of the party, fool their relatives, and amaze their friends. If you get in on the ground floor of the Abracadabra Party Plan, I guarantee you'll make enough in the next year to hire Harry Blackstone, Jr. himself to entertain at your child's next birthday party. You're probably asking, 'What kind of magic is in my Box O' Two Hundred Tricks?' Nothing but the crème de la crème."

The Box O' Two Hundred Tricks began to wriggle and twitch. It slipped from Cate's grasp and floated lazily through the air and into my waiting fingers. I tapped my wand on the side, and the plastic wrap split down the middle and squirmed off. I removed the lid and took out a plastic egg vase—a standard trick in any beginner's magic kit. Lifting the cap off the vase, I showed that it was empty. I removed the cap again, and proudly displayed a white egg in the vase. "Presto. The appearing fake plastic egg. Like magic."

No one applauded. "And that's only one o' the two hundred tricks. Here's number two—the Astounding Linking Rings. Let me assure you that these rings are absolutely ungimmicked . . . even though I can't let anyone examine them."

And so it went for the next five tricks, each one less amazing than the last. Although my audience shifted wearily in their seats, no one hurried me along. They were too uneasy about why I'd summoned them here. Jack continued his card shuffling. Nikki struggled to pay attention, but soon began thumbing through the Mystic Isle pamphlet. Zehme had seemed to grudgingly admire my rip-off of his company's idea, but that soon wore thin as I did one rinky-dink trick after another.

Posar was the first to crack. It happened as I was showing him a little plastic cube with colored spots. I put the cube in a box and claimed my "X-ray vision" would tell me which color he chose. When I asked Posar for the eighth time to "pick-a-color-any-color," he crashed his fist down on the empty metal chair beside him.

"Enough, enough . . . I can't take it anymore! What kind of sadist are you? Christ, I thought auditioning rock acts was torture."

"No need to get upset, Milan," I said. "This is nothing new to any of you. According to the records of Renaissance, Inc. everybody here has attended one of their sales meetings. And, of course, Lester Zehme, the man who started the company, has attended many, many more."

Sensing someone staring me in the back, I looked behind at the portrait of Griffin Page. I shifted a few inches to the side and felt better. "The Abracadabra Party Plan isn't much different than what you'd hear at one of Zehme's meeting, except it throws in a lot more entertainment."

"Two hundred bad tricks worth o' entertainment," Nikki said.

"Like Renaissance, my presentation includes all the hooey about the grand things man can achieve when working in harmony with others. But the similarity ends there. I also talk about the darker side of existence—the cowardly, ugly acts that man sometimes commits when working alone . . . in secret."

I dropped the X-ray vision cube into my box o' tricks. The first and last meeting of the Abracadabra Party Plan had just ended in utter failure. I wouldn't get a single recruit for my new company. But a sales meeting of a different nature was just beginning.

"Ladies and gentleman," I said, "I'd like to wrap up my meeting with a short talk entitled 'Murder is Bad Business.' I assure you that it won't be as boring as those tricks. As you know, since everyone here played in the poker game a few nights ago, you are all suspects in the murder of Lisa South."

I paused and studied each of their faces. Everyone concealed his reactions well.

Like good poker players.

CHAPTER TWENTY-EIGHT

Sullivan continued to fiddle with his cards, still hoping he'd somehow end up in a poker game tonight. When I began talking again, he shuffled more quietly. I dumped the contents of my Box O' Two Hundred Tricks into my valise and tilted the box to show it was empty.

"Everybody here had a motive for killing Lisa South. Take Jack Sullivan, for example. His gambling habit is out of control. He owes a ton of money to lenders whose collection methods are a bit severe, to say the least. It's not hard to imagine Lisa South taking Jack by surprise while he was making off with her artwork and jewelry. He could have panicked and shot her."

I pulled several handfuls of dollar bills out of my Box O' Tricks, letting them flutter to the floor. Jack stopped shuffling and looked at me with pink, sunken eyes. He wet his lips and looked for a long time at the puddle of money at my feet. For a moment, I thought he might scoop it up. He cleared his throat, riffled his cards, and said, "I won't argue that I'm always on the lookout for cash. It's equally true that I take quick advantage of any opportunities that drop in my lap. But there are a dozen easier ways to raise cash than by fencing hot goods. A thief, I'm not."

I nodded, indicating that his point was well taken. I said, "By the way, Jack, if you expect us to play with *those* cards, think again. You just stacked the four aces on top, didn't you?" He smiled proudly, not the least embarrassed that I had caught him out.

Again showing my box empty, I pulled out a children's coloring book. I flipped the pages, showing all black and white illustrations. I snapped my fingers and fanned the book again.

163

The pictures were now bursting with color. I crushed the book into a lumpy packet. I uttered a magic word and unfolded it. It had turned into the full edition of a daily newspaper. I opened the paper to the Personals section of the classified ads.

"Nikki Beacham runs an escort service," I said. "She recently discovered that Lisa South was investigating her place of work—or place of play, depending what side of the business you're on. Even though word-of-mouth is the best advertising for a dating service, Nikki often runs subtle, dignified ads in magazines and newspapers, as well as in the Yellow Pages. As long as she maintains a low profile, the law won't bother her. But the authorities tend to get unnerved when columnists like Lisa South start writing about specific dating services, naming clients. Perhaps they fear that these services will begin receiving ratings and reviews, like restaurants. Publicity in Lisa South's column would surely have brought the police down on Nikki . . . maybe even putting her out of business."

The newspaper flared into a ball of flame and vanished.

I said, "As for Milan Posar, manager of second-rate musicians, there's little that Lisa South could have written to hurt his business. The only thing—" Shrill, atonal saxophone music interrupted me. Everyone looked to the speaker on the wall, but it was still piping out the bland Dixieland music of the act following Edward's. From my Box O' Tricks, I produced a small portable radio, the source of the grating music. I turned down the volume, but the music got louder. I slammed the radio to the floor and stomped on it, but the music played on. I shouted to be heard above the cacophony. "Posar wasn't worried about what Lisa South wrote. All he cared about—as the cliche goes—was that she spelled the names of his acts right. No, Lisa South had done far worse than write bad things about Posar. She had cut him completely out of her column. No more free publicity." I pulled a blank pistol out of my magic box and fired two rounds at the radio. The music died. "Of course, being frozen out of Lisa South's column wouldn't be motive enough for murder. What really enraged Posar was that after he'd given her career its first big boost, she returned the favoring by turning her back on him, treating him like he never existed—as if he was an embarrassment to her."

Posar crossed his big arms and fumed silently. He was probably wishing he'd brought along Johnson, his bodyguard.

My gaze settled next on Lester Zehme. He was sitting up straight in his chair and couldn't have looked more confident had he brought along the whole team of attorneys who had represented him at the congressional hearings. I said, "I noticed that everyone flinched when I shot that blank gun—except you, Lester. You wouldn't happen to be more experienced with firearms than the others, would you?"

Zehme maintained his placid expression as I reached in the air. A lit cigarette popped into view, nestled between my first two fingers. Zehme frowned and said, "Please, I'd prefer you put that—" He stopped short when he realized what he was saying.

"I won't argue with you. Smoking is a lousy habit. But you're on my turf now, Zehme, and I'll put my cigarette out when I'm good and ready. It's time I checked if there's anything in my magic box for you." I felt around inside, but came out empty-handed. "I'll try again." This time I pulled out a stuffed rabbit. Next came a flowing silk streamer that changed colors every few yards. Then several bouquets of red and blue flowers. And a fifty-foot string of jewels. I shook the box, but it refused to yield more. "That stuff was pretty, but there's got to be something in here especially for you . . ." I reached in again, but pushed too hard this time. A flap sprang open in the rear. I pretended not to notice my hand sticking out the back of the box. "There must be *something* in here for Lester Zehme." I coughed noisily and repeated my last sentence.

A voice from behind the flip chart whispered loudly, "Sorry, Harry. That's it. There's nothing left."

Speaking out of the side of my mouth, I said, "Surely there's an *envelope* somewhere in the depths of my magic box."

"A what?" the whisperer asked.

"An envelope!" I shouted.

"I'll check. Ahh, here it is."

A hand waving an envelope popped up from behind the flip chart.

"No, no," I said. "Wait until I put the box in front of your hand." To no one's astonishment, I pulled an envelope out of my box. I ripped it open and read the enclosed card: "May I have your attention, please. At the count of three, the guilty party will now stand up."

"What kind of crazy parlor game is this?" Posar said, scoot-

ing far back in his seat. "Why would the guilty party all of a
sudden want to stand up?"

"Is this some sort of trick?" Nikki asked.

Sullivan did a one-handed cut with his cards and said, "My
dear, of course it's a trick. You've forgotten where you are."

I said, "One, two . . ."

Everyone positioned themselves firmly in their seats.

"Three."

The room fell dead silent. A second later, Ed McClenahan
stuck his head up from behind the flip chart. "Did it work?"

"Shhhh," I said.

Cate shook her head, as though I'd miscalculated.

But I stared directly at Lester Zehme. I watched the cool se-
renity melt from his face, replaced by an expression of dread.
He sniffed the air and his eyes grew round and buglike. "Ow!"
he yelled and shot to his feet, clutching his backside.

After he stopped hopping around, he gingerly laid a finger on
the seat of his chair and jerked it away, as if touching a sizzling
griddle.

"I appreciate your cooperation, Zehme."

"It wasn't me. This seat—"

I turned his folding chair around and pointed to a sticker on
the back. "Whoops, how careless of me," I said. "When setting
up this furniture, I accidentally mixed in a chair from The Great
Wylini's hot-seat act. Quite a coincidence that you got this par-
ticular one, seeing that you're the one who organized the poker
game . . . and killed Lisa South."

Lester Zehme looked miserable, as if he were still sitting on
Wylini's chair.

CHAPTER TWENTY-NINE

Zehme tested another seat with his fingertips, but he was hesitant to sit down again. He stared at my flip chart for a few moments, and then curiosity got the best of him. He walked over and toppled the chart to the floor, revealing Ed McClenahan hunched on a stool behind it.

"Meet Ed McClenahan," I said. "A former member of your Renaissance team. You've probably seen his creations in movies and on TV."

Zehme smiled broadly and pointed at the sheepish McClenahan. "Very nice, Colderwood. Now I know how you pulled all that junk from your 'empty' magic box."

"Yes," I said. "Just as I know how *you* did it."

"Did what?"

"Why, the murders, of course."

Zehme sat down again, crossing his legs. His posture was so rigid, I doubted that a gale-force wind could dislodge him. I imagined him sitting that way when conducting company board meetings. I handed him my Box O' Tricks and his smile grew frosty. "Since you've figured out all my magic, why not keep this as a souvenir? A reminder of things past."

A dark mustache and a wig sprang out of the box, and Zehme ducked his head out of their path. Cate caught them in mid-flight.

I said, "You wore a similar disguise the night you first visited the Mystic Isle to watch me perform . . . to size up your adversary. You used the name of Nathan Hardan, a pioneer in your style of flimflam. When I first showed Mr. Memory the pictures of the poker players, he didn't recognize anybody. But then I gave him a marking pen and asked him to draw disguises on the

167

faces—extra hair, beards, and mustaches. That's when he recognized you, Zehme.''

I displayed the picture of Zehme with the wig and mustache that Mr. Memory had inked in. ''You made another big mistake that night. You once told me that you never miss an opportunity to spread the gospel of Renaissance. But you should never have sold your chauffeur for the night, Jerome Longley, on your company. You didn't realize that while you were watching the magic show, Longley was in the Mystic Isle kitchen, extolling the virtues of Renaissance to the chef. The chef later persuaded other club employees to sign up, which eventually led to Ed McClenahan's brief encounter with your company's promises of riches. I'd love to ask Jerome Longley what he thinks of Renaissance now. But he's no longer with us.''

''Yeah, I read about it in the paper,'' Posar said. ''He killed himself in his car, didn't he? Tragic.''

''Yes, even more tragic because it wasn't suicide,'' I said.

Nikki raised her eyebrows. ''How could you tell?''

''The limo was parked on marshy ground, but there was no trace of mud on the floor of the car, or on Longley's shoes. That meant someone rendered Longley unconscious, hooked the hose to the exhaust of the limo, and drove off in another vehicle. In fact, Longley didn't even drive his car to the clearing that day.''

''And how would you know that?'' Posar asked.

''Longley was a heavy smoker, yet all the butts in the ashtray were pointing to the *right*. Whoever smoked them had sat on the passenger side. Also, a long patch of dust on the floor indicated that the seat had recently been moved back so a taller person could drive. Longley was a very short man.''

Zehme turned the Box O' Tricks upside down and shook it. Nothing fell out. ''Nice try, magic man,'' he said. ''But you forgot something. I don't know how to drive.''

''That's what your wife said. But I saw the word *lessons* written on your desk calendar. I thought at first you were taking golf lessons. But the pro at your country club says you weren't. The owner of the limo rental service told me that Longley often signed out his limo without explanation. I think Longley was giving you driving lessons. And that *you*—wearing your disguise—were the limo driver the night I played in the poker game. That driver was terrible—a downright beginner—scraping tires on the curb and pulling out in front of traffic. That driver was also an anti-smoker . . . just like you, Zehme. The way I see it, you dropped off Milan Posar at the game room and left to pick up Jack, Nikki, and me. As I recall, after we arrived that night, it took you quite a while to come out of the bathroom. What you actually did was park the limo up the road, change out of the chauffeur's uniform, double back, and crawl back through the bathroom window."

Zehme thumped the box on his knee and laughed. "Go on. I'm listening."

"Because I didn't want to be recognized, I asked Harriet O'Brien, Longley's landlady, to watch your place and report anything unusual. One of your employees was extremely rude to her." I recounted her story about burning the set of clothes. "At first I thought he was destroying evidence, perhaps bloodstains. But the real reason he burned your clothing was because they were so inundated with cigarette smoke that you considered them ruined. During your last driving lesson, you wanted to put Longley at ease, so you let him smoke . . . even though you could barely tolerate it."

"But why would I kill—what was his name again—Longley?"

"Because he wasn't as stupid as you thought . . . because after chauffeuring for those first poker games, he got suspicious and pieced together your plan, even going so far as to break in and investigate Lisa South's home, looking for clues just as I did."

"And the plan was?" Posar said.

Zehme looked at me with moist, innocent eyes. I couldn't help but admire the way he was playing the role of victim. He had something up his sleeve—not just one ace, but a whole deck of aces. Had someone tailed him here? I didn't think so. Cate had promised not to bring the group through the tunnel if any of the drivers reported being followed. So why was he so smug?

The box in Zehme's hands began to expand and contract as though breathing. Suddenly, hundreds of printed invitations—similar to the ones for the poker game—gushed out. When the barrage ended, Zehme peeked in the box. One more flew out, bopping him in the face. He rubbed his nose and winced.

"Ah, yes," I said. "The poker game. Originally, it was to be your alibi for the murder of Lisa South. You scanned the computer files of Renaissance, Incorporated, for people in this area likely to play in a high-stakes poker game. After a little investigating on your own, you narrowed that list, selecting people with possible motives for killing Lisa South. That way, if the police started asking questions, the water would be further muddied."

"But why would he kill Lisa South?" Nikki asked. "What was he afraid of?"

"At this stage of his life, not much scares Zehme. He's survived a lot of flack over the years and is almost immune to bad press. Actually, he was more worried about what Lisa South would *say*—not write—about him. He deathly feared that she would turn his wife Ali against him. Lisa South recently received pleas from friends who had lost fortunes in Renaissance. They wanted her to check into the company's workings. Zehme even visited Ms. South one evening in an attempt to dissuade her from pursuing her investigation of Renaissance. We may never know what she learned about Zehme's sleazy dealings. Her office in town was destroyed by fire. Very conveniently."

A tiny ring of smoke floated out of the box.

"To Ali, Zehme had always managed to explain away all the criticisms of his company. But he'd have been no match for Lisa South and her phenomenal gift for communicating one-on-one. In TV interviews, she easily moved grown men to tears and drew sordid confessions out of the most staid celebrities."

The box trembled and a copy of *TV Guide* popped out, landing on Zehme's lap.

"But Cate Fleming's arrival in the area almost ruined Zehme's plan. Because Cate's husband once had an affair with Lisa South, the police would naturally suspect her of murdering South . . . and Zehme knew I'd do my damnedest to clear Cate's name. But instead of abandoning his plan, he elaborated on it. To make doubly sure that Cate would be blamed for the killing, he kidnapped her and imprisoned her at the murder scene. He then kept me busy by suckering me into playing poker for what I thought was ransom money. Fooling a professional magician was a powerful ego trip for Zehme."

Nikki was staring at Zehme with awed amusement. He stopped listening to me and began glaring back at her. Nikki said, "You know, as long as I've been in the business, I'll never understand why some men with beautiful wives still pay for it."

Posar straightened up in his seat and laughed. "Him? Are you saying he pays for it?"

Zehme's face reddened.

"Lester isn't one of my customers," Nikki said. "But he's a frequent client of my other friends in the business."

Zehme tried to speak in an unctuous, one-of-the-boys tone, but his voice quavered. "Surely you understand what it's like. I've lived in a pressure cooker all my life, chasing success most of my waking hours. After a while, a man develops certain appetites for—for things he could never ask his wife to do. Why, Ali is a queen to me."

Zehme's gaze took in the whole group, but no one returned his thin smile with anything remotely resembling empathy. The only sound was Jack and his cards.

"Sullivan," Zehme said icily, "would you knock off that infernal shuffling?"

"Tell you what," Jack said, "let's cut for high card. Five hundred dollars."

"Not with *those* cards."

Cate crossed her arms and watched Zehme grip the cardboard box nervously. "Your wife was no queen to you," she said. "You treated her like another recruit for your company—someone to control and profit from. You indulged her in every way, as long as she remained in the boxed-in world you created for her. You didn't care how much pain she was in, just so her image of you remained untarnished." She paused and her burning eyes briefly looked my way. "Believe me, I know the feeling."

I didn't know if Cate was talking about her husband . . . or me. "Zehme," I said, "how long have you known of—and ignored—your wife's drug habit?"

Sullivan extended his deck to Zehme, but Zehme slapped it out of his hand, sending cards skidding along the floor. Sullivan got on his knees and began rebuilding his deck.

"You misjudged Ali," I said. "She's highly devoted to you. Even if Lisa South had portrayed you in the worst possible light, Ali would still have stuck by you. But as for her protecting a murderer—that's something different."

"You don't know anything about this crime and its—"

"Believe me, I know."

Zehme dismissed me with a wave of his hand. "Knowing isn't proving. You've got nothing. Nothing. I heard that you were snooping around Lisa South's neighborhood, but you couldn't locate the game room where we played poker. Without that game

room, there's no case. Even if you find it, you'll still have to
prove that I sneaked away from there, killed South, and returned
in time to continue playing." He tried to cross his arms defiantly,
but the magic box on his lap got in the way. Annoyed, he picked
it up in both hands. "As for your Box O' Two Hundred Tricks,
here's what I think of it."

He crushed the box between his hands and then ripped it into
jagged strips. He sorted through the hunks of cardboard, searching for gimmicks. He didn't find any. "See? There's no magic
here. Just cardboard."

I waved my hand at Zehme and a spark flew from my fingertip. It landed on the crumpled cardboard in his hands and began
to dance around the edges. The remains of the box suddenly
burst into flame. He flung the fiery ball down and stomped on
it, but the flame wouldn't die. Zehme backed off, a look of astonishment on his face.

"Funny you should mention cardboard," I said. "Because
everything around here is made of cardboard, more or less."

Zehme's eyes remained fixed on the burning box. Jack Sullivan stopped gathering his cards and glanced around. Posar turned
in his seat, looking first at the stairway and then at the rows of
dressing-room doors. Nikki stared at the double doors they had
walked through minutes before. Cate walked over to the smoking
box and ground her foot on it, extinguishing it.

"What the hell are you talking about?" Zehme said, checking
his hands for burns.

"Maybe cardboard isn't the right word," I said. "Let's call it
the theatrical equivalent of cardboard: papier maché, plastic,
foam rubber, and painted cloth. Zehme, when you said the murderer traveled from the game room to Lisa South's house, you
used the words 'from there.' You should have said 'from *here.*'
You see, my Box O' Two Hundred Tricks actually contains two
hundred *and one* tricks. I haven't shown you the last one yet.
You fooled me for a while, Zehme. But you were an amateur,
messing in a professional's game."

I crossed to the nearest dressing-room door and opened it,
revealing a blank, solid wall. "Does this wall look familiar?" I
asked. I moved to the wall speaker, which was still emitting
music, applause, and laughter. I snapped away the metal casing
around the speaker. Inside was a cassette tape recorder. I hit the
Off button and the music stopped.

I opened the whole row of doors, showing a solid wall behind each. Crossing to the opposite side of the room, I flattened my palms to the wall and shoved with all my might. It swayed a few inches. I kicked the wall sharply and it creaked, taking a nasty tilt forward.

"Now you're getting some idea why Cate asked you not to touch the walls while passing through the 'tunnel.' That tunnel was the last thing that Ed McClenahan and his men worked on last night. The paint is still wet in some places." I shoved the wall again and it sagged at a more pronounced angle.

"From his work in live television, Ed is used to moving fast, but even he admits he outdid himself with this job. You know, the saddest time for any theatrical production is striking the set."

I gave one final kick and jumped back out of the way. The wall fell forward and smacked the floor a few feet from the group, raising a cloud of dust. Behind the phony walls lay a vast, dark, open space, broken only by the wooden frame of the "tunnel" that McClenahan and his men had constructed. Barely visible against the far wall were rows of wooden pallets containing stacks of cardboard boxes. Parked next to them were three fork trucks, resembling silent metal monsters.

Nikki was the first to speak. "Where the hell are we?"

"Zehme, if you won't tell her, I will. Nikki, we're inside the warehouse of a company called Phoenix, Ltd. We sneaked in and started working last night after closing time. Because today's Saturday, the place won't be open until Monday. The limousines dropped you off at the loading dock, at the other end of the 'tunnel.' We stacked a few illusions from the Mystic Isle there to make you think you were at Al Emmons's warehouse."

I pointed at the Exit sign above a door next to the fork trucks. "On the other side of that door is a familiar sight. Would you all follow me?"

As I headed for the door, everyone but Zehme followed. He was poking his toe through the ashes of my magic box. I nodded to McClenahan, indicating that I wanted him to keep an eye on Zehme. Posar looked around at the shambles of the recreated Mystic Isle basement. He said, "Why . . . ?"

"To give Zehme a taste of what he did to all of us."

After everyone filed through the exit door, I flicked on the light. We were standing at the top of a flight of stairs. To our left was a door leading out to a small garage, the one where the limo dropped us off for the poker game. I stopped for a moment and listened. Raindrops had stopped tickling the roof of the building. While descending the steps, I looked back and saw that Zehme—still sullen—had joined us.

At the bottom of the stairway was the game room where we had played a few nights ago. Everything looked the same except for the flip chart beside the stereo system. The front sheet bore the Renaissance insignia—a coat of arms.

I said, "When Cate and I were canvassing door to door, I was struck by how many people knew of game rooms similar to this one. It finally hit me. This room was specially designed to represent the *typical* game room. Since most sales meetings are held in people's homes—quite often in basement rec rooms—this room was specially constructed as a training facility for promising sales people with Renaissance. You see, Phoenix, Limited, is a subsidiary of Renaissance, Incorporated. This warehouse is primarily a distribution center for the company's soap products. The first day I drove past Lisa South's house, I stopped in upstairs to ask directions. It took me a while to make the connection: Phoenix is the mythical bird that rises from its ashes, similar to the meaning of the word *renaissance.*"

Jack, still clutching his cards, looked wistfully at the poker table in the middle of the room.

"Zehme," I said. "You talked a few minutes ago about traveling from the game room to Lisa South's house. If you're still interested in that trip, why don't you join us? Or would you be more comfortable exiting through the bathroom window?"

Zehme didn't argue. He made a sweeping gesture with his hand that said, *"After you."* As we walked toward the stairs, he ran his hand smoothly through his hair and gave me a self-satisfied smile. He moved with the confidence of a golfer ambling down the fairway to the eighteenth hole . . . with me as his caddy.

We reached Lisa South's house in five minutes and entered the back way. I led everyone through the dark kitchen and into the living room. The only light was the flicker and glow of the television set. The group halted abruptly and someone gasped. The body of a redheaded woman was sprawled facedown on the floor in front of the TV, near the painting of the tough guy pointing the smoking gun at the blond corpse. Just like on the night of the murder.

The woman's body stirred, drawing a deep breath. The fingers came to life, its nails sinking into the carpet.

Zehme shouted "No!" He clapped his hand to his mouth, as if afraid of what he'd say next.

The body slowly rolled over and sat up. A cold voice said, "Hello, Lester . . . darling."

It was Ali Zehme, wearing Lisa's bathrobe and a red wig.

"What the hell are you doing here?" Zehme said.

"Harry invited me over to watch a little late-night TV." Her voice was steady and clear, with none of the drugged drowsiness of before. Her eyes were narrow with fury.

Zehme looked at the TV. On-screen was the image of the phony basement of the Mystic Isle. A hand flashed in front of the camera and Ed McClenahan appeared, his face filling the screen. He said, "Hey, Harry, we're going to start tearing everything down now."

I said, "Al Emmons loaned me the video system from the Mystic Isle. Good picture, don't you think? It's a wireless system that can send a signal over a short distance. If not for the surrounding hills, the reception would be even better. The camera is hidden behind that picture of Griffin Page that was hanging on the wall behind me. Page's thick eyeglasses made a perfect cover for the camera lens."

Ali, sitting on the bloodstained rug, her elbow resting on the coffee table, said, "Lester, why? How could you?"

The expression on Zehme's face reminded me of a man watching the lid slowly close on his own coffin. He glanced at the TV picture of McClenahan prying apart the fake walls with a crowbar. His eyes darted to each of the former players in his poker game and all he got in return were impassive stares. He turned back to Ali, who had removed her wig and was still asking "Why?" Her face was drawn and pale.

"You still don't have proof, Colderwood," he said. "What about the time discrepancy? You keep saying that I left the poker game, but all of us were present and accounted for during the exact time that Lisa South was shot."

"Save it for the cops, Zehme," I said.

Ali spoke slowly, her words rolling out like lumps of molten lead. "Lester, at first I didn't believe everything Harry told me.

But after sitting here, listening to what you said on the TV, I intend to tell the police what I know, including that I saw you visit Lisa South.''

I figured that long before Zehme ever entertained the idea of murder, he had an emergency plan to flee the country. I didn't doubt he had plenty of money socked away in a Swiss account. So I wasn't surprised when he made a sudden dash for the painting of the tough guy on the wall. He grabbed at the image of the gun, stubbing his fingers on the canvas and crying out in pain. A puzzled look came over him, and he reminded me of Hayden Miller, my volunteer for the disappearing flower trick. This time, I didn't feel guilty for fooling someone. I was getting my touch back.

Zehme lunged at the canvas, clawing at it like a cat attacking a piece of furniture. "Give it up, Zehme," I said. "We switched paintings. That one's a duplicate that Ed McClenahan made. The only difference is that it doesn't have a real gun—the murder weapon—concealed in it. That painting was just one of the many weapons and security devices Lisa South had hidden all over this place. You probably discovered it the first time you visited her. It took me a while to realize that an artist as committed to pacifism as James Brittain would never paint such a blatantly violent work. Cate phoned Brittain, who confirmed that his original painting had no firearm or dead woman in it. Lisa South had commissioned another artist to modify it so that a real gun could fit into the painting—like a puzzle piece. The color of the real gun was altered to make it look more like part of a painting. That's why the kidnapper's pistol reminded Cate of a cartoon gun.''

Zehme slowly retreated from the painting and sidled across the room toward the front door. When it was apparent that no one was going to try and stop him, he broke into a run, slamming his shoulders into Sullivan, sending his cards flying. Reaching the door, Zehme tugged at the knob with both hands, It was locked. His fingers danced over the locks, clicking back dead bolts and undoing chains. Finally, he wrenched open the door and dashed outside, leaving the door wide open.

Posar said, "Want me to chase him?''

I said, "No, that won't be necessary.'' Posar relaxed, happy not to have to do any running. "You know, I think Zehme secretly snickered while I was explaining my scheme to market little magic kits. But it was his company that inspired me. They're now running an offer for free magic sets on the back of their soap. All you have to do is send in a hundred wrappers. While Ed and I worked on the Phoenix warehouse set today, I found an entire case of Renaissance Soap. I felt like a ten-year-old again, dying to know what was in that free magic kit. I couldn't resist. Although it was pouring outside, I carted the whole case over here to Lisa South's house. After I peeled off the soggy wrappers, I didn't know what to do with all that soap. I hated to waste it. Then I got a great idea. You know, it rained so hard today, I bet that soap still isn't dry yet.''

I grinned when I heard Zehme scream as he slid across the wet soap bubbling over the front sidewalk of Lisa South's house.

The soap Lester Zehme had built an empire on.

CHAPTER THIRTY

We were in the basement of the Mystic Isle, the *real* basement this time. The speaker on the wall was silent and the dressing rooms were dark. The audience and entertainers had long since gone home. The police were still at Lisa South's house, sorting out the facts of the case. All of us—Cate, Milan Posar, Nikki Beacham, and Jack Sullivan—were sitting around a table at the end of the main room, sharing a bottle of Johnnie Walker. Talk was sparse. Everyone was too exhausted to admit he didn't have the energy to simply get up and go home.

Posar yawned and said, "So who was this Nathan Hardan you talked about, Harry?"

"Hardan was a businessman who pioneered the pyramid type of business Zehme modeled Renaissance after. Hardan was more than a role model to Zehme. You see, among other crack-brained ideas of the paranormal, Zehme believed in reincarnation."

"There were many parallels in their lives," Cate said. "Zehme may have actually believed that he was Hardan, reincarnated. After all, just consider the name of his company."

"Renaissance . . . meaning rebirth," Posar said.

"Exactly," I said. "The library told me that Hardan tried solving some of his problems with violence. Family members and lovers disappeared without a trace. Since Hardan had gotten away with it so easily, maybe Zehme thought he could do the same."

Nikki rubbed the bridge of her nose. "What about the time discrepancy that Zehme mentioned? He was right. We *were* all playing cards at ten-thirty, the time of the murder."

Cate said, "You've got to remember that the neighbor lady who called the cops isn't sure how long she delayed before dialing. *I'm* the one that heard the shot and established the time of death. And I was wrong.''

I tapped another cigarette from my pack. With Zehme behind bars, my desire for tobacco had quadrupled. ''I should have realized that something was wrong when Cate kept being late meeting me. Show them your watch, Cate.''

She removed her bracelet and pushed a tiny button on the side. A metal flap sprang up, revealing a watch face. ''After being late twice, I realized that my watch was slow. I thought at first that the batteries had run low, but actually the watch had been set back an hour. When the police confiscated my personal effects, they didn't notice that it had been tampered with. It looks so much like a bracelet, they didn't even realize it was a watch.''

I said, ''In addition, I noticed that Cate's arm was sore while we were at the police station. Zehme put something in her food, possibly the same stuff his wife was using. When she was unconscious, he even gave Cate an injection, just to further muddle her sense of time. Hence, the sore arm. Zehme was adept with a syringe, I saw him give an insulin shot to his cat. When Cate was unconscious, he set her watch back.''

All this talk about time caused everyone to peek at their own watches. Finishing his drink, Posar said, ''Folks, I've got a new group to audition tomorrow. They're crazy enough to think their music sounds better in the morning. If you'll excuse me . . .'' He started to get up.

''Not so fast,'' Jack said. He tossed an unopened deck of cards onto the table. ''Let's do what we came here for. The invitation did say a poker game, right? Dammit, it won't hurt to play a few hands.''

Nikki shook her head and laughed. ''You've got it bad, don't you?'' But she didn't move from her seat.

''Are you kidding?'' Posar said. ''After what happened tonight?'' But he was already checking his coat pocket for his envelope of cash. Teeth clamped together, Jack smiled and tore the cellophane from the card box. Nikki cleared the table of everything but the bottle and glasses.

I pushed my chair away from the table to stand next to Cate. Jack started to deal, pausing when he got to me. ''You in, Harry?''

''Nah. Not after the dirty tricks I pulled on you guys in our last game. On my way out, I'll remind Al Emmons that you're down here so he won't lock you in.''

Posar shrugged. ''Your sleight of hand doesn't worry us. We just won't let you deal. Fair enough?''

''There's also the question of funding. I've had a lot of expenses in the past days and . . .''

Cate handed me an envelope from her purse. ''I forgot about this. You can use it if you want.''

I lifted the flap and saw a stack of new bills. ''Where'd this come from?''

''You might say I had a dream that came true.''

I refused to believe it. ''You're kidding. The lottery?''

''Yep. Remember the numbers from the dream book? They hit.''

Cate relished my look of amazement. I tried to give the money back, but she shook her head and said, ''No, I insist. There isn't a lot there. Just enough to keep you in the game a few hands. And after you lose it all, we can go back to the hotel. I'd like to finish telling you about my dream.''

Because Cate's method of winning the money violated everything I stood for, the bills in the envelope felt like ill-gotten gain. She had won it by pure luck, so I felt almost obligated to wager it away in a poker game—where psychology, not luck, dictates the winner.

As I sat back down, Cate stationed herself on the edge of the sofa. After I was dealt my first hand, I glanced back at Cate and grinned. She looked wary, perhaps now regretting giving me the envelope. ''Don't worry,'' I said. ''Just a few hands, win or lose, and then we'll celebrate your freedom in style.''

But my words had a familiar ring . . . like the promises of a long time ago. Promises to prove to Cate that she was just as important to me as my career.

From the moment I picked up the cards, I felt a comfortable glow. The same glow as when I'm onstage facing hundreds of people, armed only with silk scarfs and billiard balls and shiny coins.

My pile of money grew steadily until it no longer fit in the envelope. No matter what cards I was dealt, I found ploys to crush my opponents. With each new hand, Cate's promise to tell me about her dream grew dimmer. My whole world was reduced to a round table, fifty-two cards, and a bottle of Johnnie Walker that had strangely become tasteless.

The poker game lasted more than a few hands.

When I finally looked at my watch, I wondered if someone had tampered with it, too. Surely it wasn't that late. I felt bone-weary—yet relaxed—similar to when the curtain rings down on my act for the final time.

I looked around for Cate. The sofa was empty. I drained the rest of my glass, "Anyone see Cate?"

The poker players answered with indifferent shrugs, angry at the interruption. "I gotta go," I said, folding my bills into a thick roll.

As I'd expected, they protested that I was taking all their money. There were jealous murmurs about how lucky I was to-night. Sore losers, I thought. I was too tired to point out that the very idea of luck was the downfall of most gamblers. Luck was as much a figment of the imagination as Zehme's belief in reincarnation.

I checked inside each dressing room, but I didn't find Cate. I had become a victim of illusion myself. If anyone hates being fooled, it's a magician . . . even when it's his own fault.

In Mr. Memory's dressing room, I saw that he had forgotten his checkbook and a set of keys. I shook my head and smiled. There was hope for him yet.

I roamed the stage area upstairs in search of Cate. I called out her name.

"Harry?"

I turned and saw Buzz Kerns standing in the wings. Tucked under his arm was a file folder overflowing with computer paper. "I've got bad news," he said. "After extensive computer analysis, the graphologist, the astrologer, and the numerologist concur that *Cate* wrote that note. I'm afraid there is no kidnapper. Cate is the guilty one. We have no choice now but to throw ourselves on the mercy of the court."

I patted him on the shoulder and promised to meet him at the D.A.'s office tomorrow. After he left, I strolled over to the lighting panel and turned up the footlights. I walked onstage, stopping at the edge of the stage apron. Squinting, I looked out at the empty chairs and tables, remembering the times that Cate and I had trod these very boards. I recalled the many times she'd accused me of being so wrapped up in fooling people that I didn't care about people for their own sakes. I patted the wad of bills in my pocket. Maybe she was right.

"She's probably back at the hotel room," I said aloud. "Yeah, sure. She's waiting there right now."

Sometimes the best illusions are the ones that magicians pull on themselves. It would be easy to dial the hotel room. I found a quarter in my pocket, but didn't call my own bluff. I decided to wait to learn the truth.

I stood for a few moments at the edge of the stage, waiting for the footlights to fill me with the usual warmth and excitement. But their magic didn't work tonight. I tried hard not to think about my next job—parading around in convenience store parking lots in an old man's costume, handing out free lollipops and yardsticks.

Letting the stage lights burn, I switched on the house lights and cranked up every spotlight until the hall was ablaze.

And the damn place still felt cold.